Dust covered, sun baked 'til cracked, we find ourselves sitting in a saddle molded by our sweaty weight, riding to that third hill over to the west, eyes holding the horizon, senses keen in all directions. Tom Sheehan brings us to the heart and soul of the American West, tobacco chewing and spitting, among the cowboys and Indians. John Wayne would have won an Oscar award acting in a Sheehan western.

Tom Sheehan knows the glint in the eye of the low rays of day, and the sparking embers of the soul as it sets to the west. The rawhide of a man who sleeps endless nights under that big sky, a mother's heart-wrung ache, the lightning on the lonely mountainside, saloon brawls in the valley. Nostrils flare, at the ready. Need speaks wordlessly and kinship ignites. Sheehan knows the scalping in the head and the hand, the clash for territory, and the claim that no one can stake where all men beg for the same mercy from land and sky. Steinbeck, get ready to draw your gun.

> -Dianne Buccheri, Publisher *OCEAN* Magazine and *EARTH
> OCEAN SOUL* Photographer

Once again Tom Sheehan circles the range, this time re-finding the American character in the living shadows of the historical West, both beside and within the Indian nations whose unmarked graves shape our selected history and the decencies and flaws in re-created lives. Sheehan doesn't compromise and he doesn't flinch.

> -Don Junkins (author of *Buster's
> Book* and *Burning the Leaves*)

The Nations is an extremely good, very well written book about the life and struggles during the Native American time in our history. The author, Tom Sheehan, has a knack for vivid descriptions of life in this time and for making the reader feel that he is captured in that very moment of the story.

I was completely engaged by Tom's intimate description of the mountain pool scene between Jobie Trask and Blue Wing, Maiden of the pool, and her beautiful, elegant and curvaceous body. At the end of that story, I too wanted to be Jobie Trask.

-C. Warren, Bangor, Maine

Author Tom Sheehan's recent Indian tales deserve special attention. As a reader and viewer of decades filled with variations of Tonto in Indian portrayals, Sheehan gives us hope for a realistic view of honorable people who deserved far better treatment than they got from this, their own country. I am especially impressed with the sensory details. Readers can see, hear, touch, smell and taste the atmosphere. Most important, when you read Sheehan, you will feel genuine compassion- and want to thank the writer as I just attempted to do.

-Maureen Lynch Edison, North Shore
Community College

The Nations

Thomas F. Sheehan

Pocol Press
Clifton, VA

POCOL PRESS
Published in the United States of America
by Pocol Press
6023 Pocol Drive
Clifton, VA 20124
www.pocolpress.com

Publisher's Cataloguing-in-Publication

Sheehan, Thomas F., 1928-

> The Nations / Thomas F. Sheehan.
> p. cm.
> ISBN: 978-1-929763-60-3

1. Native Americans--Fiction. 2. Western stories. 3. Indians of North America—Fiction. I. Title.

PS3569.H39216

813.54 --dc23   2014948234

Library of Congress Control Number: 2014948234

ABOUT THE COVER

"Passage," or "He Who Watches," is the title of the cover painting by Thomas F. Sheehan, Jr. (deceased), who saw it as a directed walk to an assigned reservation by an elder Native American. The man is a Kiowan (from the Kiowa word Kó-i, plural Kó-igu, meaning Káyowe man), which says he is leaving the old ways clad in his winter buckskin garb, while keeping his Kiowa wooden lance at hand, a sign of eternal belief in his way of life. The lance serves as a ceremonial instrument as well as a means of obtaining food from wild life hunting.

Cover arranged by Jamie Sheehan. Painting by Thomas Sheehan, Jr. Cover designed by Amelia Hetrick.

ACKNOWLEDGEMENTS

The author wishes to acknowledge the editors of various internet sites, such as *Perpetual Magazine,* that have bitten the dust but where some of these stories appeared in earlier versions (and sometimes with different titles), the editor of *Frontier Tales Magazine* and the editor of *Rope and Wire Western Magazine.* Much of my computer log information on submission and acceptance records was lost when my computer contracted a serious virus.

Preface

My early reading material, and thus my reading habits, in the 1930s of the Depression era, where it seemed I was always hungry for the next meal and the next issue to read, came in the soft, pulpy shape of dime magazines on the shelves of variety stores and local drug stores where these magazines crowded the shelves in a corner or the secret section behind the door where a child like me, silent, diminutive, used to games of hide 'n' seek, could have unpaid privacy while reading...

The westerns, especially, grasped my attention for several reasons; the country expanding west was the core of the stories. On display were the trail masters and wagon masters, the brave and legendary scouts who moved alone against huge odds, the mountain men being a rare breed on their own missions, the lawmen in great singular stands against depraved outlaws, and the regular flights from Indian war parties big and small that looked for game as much as they looked for those who were invading their territory.

But as easily as these cast of characters found deep sympathy in me with their heroics, unique traits and capabilities, their displays of wit and courage, there suddenly streamed into my finite and partially closed mind, but clearly into my consciousness even at a tender but influential age, that words, and views of all things western, were being understood by me *between the lines,* where questions began to rise about treatment meted out to Native Americans ... all over the place.... those whose tribes, whose Nations, had been here for thousands of years, from who knows how long before the Anasazi or Pueblo people roamed free on the Colorado Plateau, before the Sioux grew big enough to have their own divisions/tribes/heroes or my hometown of Saugus, MA was home to the Almouchiquois, as named by early explorer Samuel de Champlain and John Smith. The Almouchiquois consisted of different groups living in regions between Saugus (Rumney Marsh), Naumkeag (Salem), Agawam (Ipswich), Newichawannock and Piscataqua (Portsmouth area), and

Aucocisco (Portland), they all spoke a similar language and were allied to one another. The Almouchiquois were devastated by a series of war raids on them by eastern people, the Tarrentines or Micmacs, who lived in eastern Maine, New Brunswick, and Nova Scotia ... and disease. Solid traces remain: Montowampate is on our town seal and the Saugus High School yearbook is titled *The Tontoquonian,* for Tontoquon, born between 1650-1660 to Petaghuncksq (called Cicely or Su-George), wife of the Sagamore Petagh. (From Saugus native and State of Maine geologist Thomas Weddle's *John Tontohqunne, Cicely's Son.)*

Generally when gathered in the class of Native Americans, most Indian tribes/nations were not allied under a leader unless drawn together for survival/attack such as the Battle of Little Big Horn, which wreaked havoc on the army. Other battles, actions, campaigns, were moments of carnage and inhuman warfare levered by politics, greed, and propitious gains on the side of the government, its leaders, backers. In spite of grievous wounds, many simple, personal friendships were formed, challenged, brought to fruition between native people and some of those bent on exploiting the whole of the west.

The Nations suffered most seriously when they were separated from food sources. The losses reached into each tribe, each village, each campsite when such incursions ran onto hunting territories or sacred burial grounds. The Native Americans reacted as all peoples react for such desecration; a mass move to arms, for battle, for survival.

The wounds were many... The Sand Creek Massacre, Wounded Knee, the Colorado War, the Mankato executions, images of the down-trodden marching off to poor or distant reservations ... each instance generated by the greedy clutches of politicians, profane military leaders and hungers for riches held by somebody else. I didn't find these wounds: they found me.

TABLE OF CONTENTS

Varden DeNoncoeur woke up on a shelf of a cave, in absolute darkness. Perhaps, he thought, the depth of a tunnel, blackness being as thick as a winter coat about him, and not a glint of light showing itself. He had not experienced such darkness because he always knew stars, moon, campfire, torch, or a reflection of last light. He tried to remember the last thing he had seen, but it would not come back to him. There had been noise, lots of noise, like screaming or yells from two separate places. It might have been a chant, a Crow chant, distorted in its hearing.

He was dressed in deerskin from head to foot, with a fur coat bundled with his shoulder pack, leather boots drawn tightly with rawhide string. A single shot pistol was thrust in his belt and a keen knife was slung in a sheath of leather hanging from his shoulder. For distance shooting in a hunt for food, he carried a long rifle. He was rarely separated from his rifle.

About him he gathered the last things he had known for sure, like facts collected for a trial, and not yet presented:

He'd been months on this search, his curiosity consuming him about the Crow stories of the god of the mountains; it had found in him a thirst and an agreement of some of the tenets of that Indian belief, which he wanted to experience for himself.

Other than that he knew the following about his situation:

He was in Montana, after leaving Manitowaning in Canada and Monroe Mary and their son Jacques in a small cabin on the edge of the big lake. Her squaw mother, Two-Tongues-Wise, who had lost her man in an avalanche, was with her.

With great help and great patience, he spoke the Crow language, taught him by Two-Tongues-Wise and One-Who-Speaks-Two-Sides, her elderly father.

He was in the mountains.

He had found a secret entrance to the heart of a mountain he had been searching for.

It was one of two mountains he had seen from a great distance, but he could not say which one he was now inside … he had been underground for such a long while on his latest deep-earth search, for that is where the search would end, not on a mountain but in a mountain, in the heart of a mountain.

And last of all, and perhaps most important, he had been in Crow country for more than two months of his travel, and he had been well-prepared to speak in the Crow language from Two-Tongues-Wise and One-Who-Speaks-Two-Sides who had been saved from sure death when trapped under a fallen stone. His leg was amputated by Doctor Kinsell, a friend of DeNoncoeur's family.

In short order the Crow language had come to DeNoncoeur from trees and rocks kissed by wind and from the edge of water where the wind parted company, and from the footprints of bear and coyote and wolf where the land accepted them like they were signatures of those who had passed by, in whose tracks he often stood. He was tuned into them even though he was in flight from two Crows chasing him on foot. He heard their names called back and forth as if trying to frighten him, Hides-inside-Rocks and Eyes-See-Where-Night-Goes. And both names he knew meant a place deep inside-the-mountain … maybe that is where he was at this minute, at the foot of a god of the mountains. History, he believed, sat around him in the blackness, and he could not imagine it being anything else.

A few days earlier, crawling through endless tunnels and apertures and following a route of caves through the innards of the mountain, he had heard the talk coming from behind him or below him. They, like all Crows, were relentless.

The words they spoke, both in Crow and frequently using words in his own tongue to describe him, seemed to give away secrets of the mountain, secrets that no white man might ever have heard. DeNoncoeur felt privileged. He was in range. He was close to the dream of sharing.

"The captured light comes loose soon," one said, and the other replied, "And it departs almost too quickly as it descends into the heart of the mountain. There is only so much illumination for such a short time. It would take the time of hundreds of moons to make these signs to Montowanta we see before us. And hundreds of ancestors spent their time here, waiting for the one sign to assist them in their tasks of respect."

There was silence before he spoke again, saying, "We know you cannot go out and come back in between the holy lights from afar. And there are no torch remnants here and no ashes or dust from a fire. All the signs to the god have been made in the captured light of the sun. The elders told us we would come to this and should never despair. We must go back and get our supplies and wait here until Devil-on-Two-Feet shows. Perhaps he comes tomorrow or tonight, for this must be what he has been looking for all this time. Let us go now and we will be back before all is black outside and in here at the same time."

While the two braves were gone, DeNoncoeur scoured for rocks and loose boulders, piled them at the edge, and set them tenuously atop one another so that with little effort they would all cascade down the wall of the cave. If nothing else, the cascade of rocks would send his own sign to the braves awaiting his arrival.

In a matter of hours, he heard them coming back to settle in for the wait.

"Well, Eyes-See-Where-Night-Goes," said Hides-inside-Rocks, "we should be adding our signs to the god, but we are not so gifted. We are just protectors for the God of Two Mountains. If Devil-on-Two-Feet, enters this tepee of Montowanta, we shall bury him in here. He shall not carry the heart of Montowanta away from here even in the smallest piece he might try to steal."

Later, after the Crow braves had eaten in darkness, DeNoncoeur heard a different sound, not the noise of men moving, but something strange and full of promise, of enlightenment. The mountain did not shake but there was a moving presence all around him. It emanated off the walls. Perhaps, he thought, a revelation of the true mountain or the true god. An image came to him of the old iron stove in Manitowaning warming up in its promise. On raw days it carried its own blessing and now and then was as red as a sunset between peaks.

Hides-inside-Rocks said, "Get ready. The captured light comes soon. The air gets warm with the new respect as the mountain itself awaits the light, welcomes it, like a squaw welcomes her man back from the buffalo hunt."

There, in the midst of blackness, below him and his fellow brave, and below Varden DeNoncoeur hiding above them on a deep shelf, a light came rising as if from a great depth. It came up through a pool of water in the heart of darkness and it lasted only for a short time. But it threw light outward in that darkness and DeNoncoeur saw magnificent etchings or drawings or paintings on the inner walls of one of the two mountains of one god. The decorations, or signs of respect, covered the walls and must have told the story of infinity and the beginning of the Crow existence when the noble black bird first flew out of the darkness of the mountain carrying all the blackness elsewhere in the world for a full half day before it flew back again at dusk.

The sudden illumination made DeNoncoeur think about the source of the light that dropped perfectly vertical out in front of him and the two Crow braves. He suddenly realized that it came from overhead, directly overhead, and it could only be a transfer from sunlight coming down a shaft into the heart of the mountain. He wondered how many days in the year the light would last. How long it lasted on other days, if it did last any longer on another occasion. And he imagined no other light source was allowed for this dedication and honor by which the drawings or etchings or paintings might be completed, accomplished, the Indian way; it was a testament to the God of Two Mountains, one light from the sky, where that god sat above all the tribe, above all the Nations.

DeNoncoeur held his breath an interminably long time, the amazement building in him, the passage of eons of times sifting through him swiftly, him trying to measure the impossible, and finally yielding to the realization that all this about him, about the two Crow braves below him, was as old as mankind itself and only took one's faith to know it.

DeNoncoeur waited in the darkness on the high shelf of the cave, not daring to eat any food, afraid the aroma would reveal his hiding place. Then the short, silent, explosion of light happened again a few hours later, as if it had slanted into the cave from another direction, another angle. He envisioned the passage of the sun overhead and figured there had to be more than one shaft into the heart of the mountain, more opportunities to pay homage to the god. He wondered how many shafts would be needed to pay proper respect.

DeNoncoeur heard Eyes-See-Where-Night-Goes say, "This day already, Montowanta allows us to pay our respects for the second time in one sun. How wise he is, knowing the difficulties in getting here. We must sit and make sure that Devil-on-Two-Feet does not disturb this place. His skills have been sharpened by a guiding hand."

"The god's work is not yet done for this day, as the elders say," Hides-in-Rocks said, and DeNoncoeur could envision him nodding his head.

Getting groggy from his adventure, DeNoncoeur, feeling like he would soon fall asleep, worried about snoring. He did not fear the two braves might climb to his hiding place, for the wall was too steep and too smooth. But they might trap him in here, starve him into capture. In order to capture him, or kill him, they'd have to go back out all the way to find the other entrance he had taken. That would take time, lots of time.

He tried to keep his mind alert, his hearing sharp, but reality began to fade. Finally, his blanket on the shelf under him, his head on his shoulder pack, DeNoncoeur drifted off to sleep. In a dream that had continued from other nights, he dreamed of Monroe Mary back in Manitowaning, on the other side of the great lake in Canada. Endlessly he had dreamed of her and the God of Two Mountains, both of which were now so entwined in his life he could not think of one without the other entering the same thought, sharing the same image.

In one dream, as he reached for Monroe Mary beside him, his hand found the God of Two Mountains sitting right beside him. For a moment he almost saw the god's face, but knew it was not true, for Monroe Mary's face sat in its place, her eyes like the small pretty blue flowers crawling on the bank of a stream, the dawn's pink glow moving on her cheeks, her fair red lips curving as soft as a crescent moon just rising over a peak of white. When he looked again, the God of Two Mountains, without a face, pointed to the southwest, always to the southwest.

He almost said aloud, "But I am there. In the southwest. In the heart of one of your mountains. His voice would not come. Instead, a cough issued from deep inside his chest. He gagged on the cough, and heard the Crow braves abuzz with anxiety.

"He is here," Hides-in-Rocks said. "He is here. Devil-on-Two-Feet is here,"

"Quick," said Eyes-See-Where-Night-Goes, "he is above us. When the captured light comes, we must look for a way up."

"Why has the God of Two Mountains not punished him, the intruder? Is that what he has left us to do, to punish him in our way?"

Varden DeNoncoeur saw no better chance than to act at that moment and he pushed one stone out of the pile he had made. With a thunderous roar, right on top of the words from Hides-in-Rocks, the mass of boulders and stones and sharp remnants of stone, thus freed of their bind, came crashing down into the chamber of the holy light from above. The cascade was accompanied by a host of echoes that rang into and out of other caverns and tunnels in an ominous whirlwind of threat to the Crows in the chamber.

The two braves scattered, believing that the God of Two Mountains had been disturbed and had acted this way, by threatening their mission and making this deadly sound, the way the whole mountain would sound if it descended from its highest point on top of them.

DeNoncoeur heard the last sound from them as he waited in the darkness to see if he had set loose other parts of the mountain. Swiftly there came into his memory the single, loud yell causing the snow avalanche that fatally buried Two-Tongues-Wise's man, the father of Monroe Mary and the grandfather of Jacques DeNoncoeur. Now that yell sat in the silence of the mountain.

He slept again, waited an appreciable time in silence, and then retrieved a rope from his gear, looped it on a large rock and slid down the sheer wall in the continuing darkness. Something told him to hurry; he did not know how long he had slept.

But the mountain, as it had on the earlier occasions, was making an announcement of its own, a change in temperature, a "feeling" or "sense of feeling" coming off the rock wall. He thought of how heat made changes in the property of dough, how a clutch of white mud became a loaf of delicious bread.

Quickly, even in the darkness, he was at the edge of the small pool. Dipping his hands into the water, he cupped a handful, brought it to his mouth, drank it off, and filled the cup of his hands again and stood up. The temperature changed again. Energy was loosed, and the shaft of captured light suddenly leaped down the shaft, glistened into his cupped hands, and reflected that energy in a blast of illumination that shone on every surface of the cavern.

And that included his whole person, lit up as if hit by a bolt of lightning.

There, the two Crow braves, standing in awe in the blast light, motionless and dumbfounded, saw Devil-on-Two-Feet catch the signal of respect from the God of Two Mountains as the captured light again flashed off his hands. They fell to their knees as the light lit up again the entire interior of the cavern as it emanated from his cupped hands, just as if a holy lamp had been lit by him, on him, for him.

"This," DeNoncoeur said aloud, not afraid of anyone ever hearing him, "is the moment of miracle for me, in the heart of a mountain where the sun of the god touched my hands. Wait until I tell Two-Tongues-Wise and One-Who-Speaks-Two-Sides, that I have known their god, that he spoke to me this way. And wait until I tell Monroe Mary and Jacques that I have already been where I will take them in their time, to this holy place."

Lakota Betty

It had been about 20 years since the ignominious raid on the Indian village at River Hill had taken place. The army captain, Gregory Merton, who led the raid, and all his officers, and supposedly all but one of the enlisted ranks, had been killed in later actions. The sole known enlisted rank not dead was a retired sergeant, Martin O'Keeffe, who told the discharging officer on the day he left the army that there was one other witness to the raid, and he hoped she was still living.

"How do you know that, Sergeant," the officer said, his head hanging low at the thought of River Hill that must have been weaving through his mind.

O'Keeffe, the officer saw for the first time, had visible scars from his wars, scars that hardened his face, said he was resolute, committed, and durable. One thin line, slightly red on one cheek, said he had been most likely in a hand-to-hand situation at least once in his career. A small knob on the sergeant's nose gave him the familiar characteristic of a pugilist who had received a high hard fist, also at one time, on or off duty.

"I saw her, sir," O'Keeffe said, "a little blonde girl hiding in the hollow of a large tree." The livid scene of River Hill came back in a rush. "She was no Indian with that head of hair, but she was part of that encampment. Most likely taken from her people at one time." When he closed his eyes he could see her again, the deep blue of her eyes full of terror, the mass of blonde hair saying she was not an Indian.

"Did Captain Merton know about her?" His face still had embarrassment written all over it; O'Keeffe thinking the flush was highly uncomfortable for an officer.

"I wouldn't tell that man a word about her, sir, then or now, even if he was here with us. If he stood here with a blade at my throat, I'd not tell him about her. And I know I was the only one who saw her. We were eye to eye for the sorriest moment in this life. I've seen her every night since then."

"That's a credit to you, sergeant, that you didn't give her away. It's a horrible stain on the army, the whole incident. But I wish you luck wherever you go, and I sincerely hope none of this follows you. From what I have heard over the years, you're the lone survivor, at least on the army side."

He shook O'Keefe's hand and dismissed him, from the room, from the army, from service to his new country, in the company of an attending corporal, the company clerk, who sometime down the line, perhaps in another outfit, or on another assignment, shot off his big mouth about Sergeant Martin O'Keefe and the lone witness of the River Hill massacre, a blonde girl.

As fast as ponies and horses allowed, the word spread at first to army posts all through the west, through towns and settlements on the edges of grass, mountains and rivers, through the ranks of army Indian scouts, and finally, as if demanded by the notoriety of the deed, moved slowly but consistently into every Indian village north and west of the Mississippi River.

Both sides of the incident were caught up in the after-shock.

In the small Montana town of Clusterville, squatting like a postage stamp on a quick turn on the Powder River, one of the weekly visitors to the general store was a gorgeous and most regal blonde Indian maiden who insisted her name was Lakota Betty. Her language, in English and Sioux, was impeccable to the tuned ear, and she often carried on long conversations with both townspeople and Indians of her village, which sat near rapids about 20 miles upriver.

When the story about the "Indian blonde survivor of River Hill" first surfaced in Clusterville, Jed Bolyx of the general store told every customer who'd listen to him about the survivor, and what he believed was his own private secret about the little blonde witness. That part he savored in revealing, because it was so very special in his mind.

"Said she was about 6 or 7 years old, they do, when them rotters shot the place up and everyone in it including babies and women." If he was outside the store he would have spit on the ground to show his disgust.

He was talking to the banker, Adam Flinkfelt, who tried to dust him off. "You know, Jed, people hear you talking like that and you might lose some customers. Injuns killed a lot of folks." Flinkfelt's suit, high fashion for a small town, had pointy collars, a rich orange grain running through it, and his shoes with button buckles would not sit well on a horse.

"Oh, yeah, and where'll they go then, Adam, and where'll they bank their money when they hear you say them soldiers was heroes for what they done that day?"

9

Bolyx felt good standing his ground, and bankers, he said to himself, always was a tricky lot to begin with.

"Well, I didn't say it like that, did I?" The banker was retreating in a hurry, dollar signs and decimal points tossing their weight around.

"What's more," Bolyx added, "when I tell Lakota Betty when she comes in next time, which most likely will be the day after tomorrow, she'll climb up on that horse of hers and have at it with you. Betcha bottom dollar on that, and you won't stand a chance with that girl sitting a horse the way she does and right out in front of your place of business, handling two languages the way she does. The girl's a miracle. Believe me."

The banker had no idea at all what the grocer was telling him.

"Can't we back off on this, Jed? You make me uncomfortable. If my business goes south on me, where do you think yours is going? Don't miss out on any good business, Jed." Then, like in a swap deal, he let out his own secret in the clipped fashion he used when doing so. "The army's coming. Coming this way. They're going to open a new post near here. Right near here. On the river. Getting Linderfall's land. Maybe a regiment. Maybe more. That'll be great for your business. For mine too. We have to cover the ground behind us. Common sense says so. It has to tell you that. Listen. Hear the business move."

His eyes flickered in detail signs.

Bolyx recognized the delivery as soon as Flinkfelt started. It was the same way he opened up about Sarah Winslow when he said, "She's not what you think. Maybe what you hope. I'd say that. How she skips Monday's wash. When John's downriver. Makes up for it on Tuesday. Before he gets back. But Monday's are free. She's the old Sarah then. Just on Mondays though." He'd closed his eyes then, his soul torn in half. After all, he could only hold in so much.

Bolyx hoped he didn't have such weaknesses, though it was no time to search, to measure. His daughter worked a corner display into focus. His wife, two years near infirm, in the bed above his head, still held him with steady reins.

The door opened and Lakota Betty, in colors that might blast the eyes of some men, stood in the doorway, a black stallion tied to the hitch rail behind her. The black stallion set off a frame around Lakota Betty's blonde hair, as golden and as rich as a whole field of corn with a sun riding on it as glorious as glory could be. Those tresses rode down one cheek as if they had been painted on her in a studio, and the other half of those long tresses fell over one shoulder like a cape tossed on her red-orange-purple dress the likes of which no other woman in Clusterville could or would wear.

Bolyx shivered in primal recognition of the ultimate female, the ultimate woman. The dress sheathed her, letting shadows run where they ought, along with his mind. She smiled at him, perhaps reading his thoughts, and ignored the banker completely. Bolyx understood. He smiled back.

In a quick turn to look at Bolyx's daughter, she said, "Hello, Melva, that looks nice."

She turned back to the counter and the open-mouthed grocer standing at attention. "Tell me, Mr. Bolyx, what do you hear about a soldier who was at the River Hill massacre? The one they say is still alive. Tell me what his name is. Where he is? Why is word just coming about him all this time later?"

Bolyx, without pausing, said, "I heard that he was recently discharged from the army after serving all this time. His name is Martin O'Keeffe, an Irish transplant. He was a sergeant a long time and was discharged a few months ago at Fort Baker."

He had to say more. He didn't know how to say what had filled his mind since he heard the first word about O'Keeffe.

And Lakota Betty, much like a teacher in a quiz session, tipped her head, smiled at him, and drew it out practically all the way, letting it sit right there in his mouth, all framed up and ready for the world.

"They say he saw a little blonde girl hiding in a hollow tree trunk at River Hill and let her be. He believed she was not an Indian because of her blonde hair, like yours." He dropped his head, lifted his gaze and looked her right in the eyes. "Said he can remember her eyes to this day. That they have haunted him every day from the sorriest day of his life. Those are his words, as exact as they can be, from all reports, but you know how such things can get twisted."

Lakota Betty was still smiling at him, so he said, "Do you want me to try to find out where he is for you?"

"Oh, no," Lakota Betty said, "we have our ways. Always have." She nodded to Bolyx and his daughter, ignored the banker and walked out of the store.

When she mounted the big black stallion, her hair catching the sun, the dress shining its shape to a discerning eye, she was regal, and

11

the horse pranced as part of the show … a lost white girl, a blonde Indian maiden, complexity on horseback, a rhythmic, colorful entity, a child grown up to be a queen without a throne.

On the Carter-O'Keeffe Ranch about 60 or so miles from Fort Baker, new and permanent home to Morgan Carter and his uncle, Martin O'Keeffe, the two men sat on the porch of their cabin slowly becoming, day by day, the ranch house of the C/O Ranch. More than 100 head of cattle grazed in a fenced pasture of 50 or so acres, half a dozen goats tromped the grass in another smaller plot of fenced-off ground, one pig, as fat as a dog house, looked about ready to say goodbye to his sty. Some birds had already nested in the eaves of the barn, and an owl, at a distance, seemed to want to join in the darkening solitude of the ranch proper.

Long shadows had settled along the ground and the large barn, four times as big as the cabin, threw its shadow onto the grass. From inside the barn the two men on the porch could hear the chanting of four stray Indians who had found a home with the "new ranchers. One of them was Pawnee, one a Cherokee and the two older Indians were Lakota Sioux. Each of them had more than one name and it was according to whom they were talking which name they went by or were addressed. In general, on the ranch in the company of Carter or O'Keeffe, they were Twisted Water, Broken Feather, Tall Answer and So Sioux Said, the last being the oldest of them and one whose smile had not faded since his first meal in the barn and plenty of soft, dry hay to sleep on. He was the only Indian Martin O'Keeffe ever heard laugh.

Young Carter, rescued from a most dull life of working for someone else, by an uncle he had only seen twice in his life, sat back in one of the two porch chairs he had made after the barn was built. Reveling in evening' sudden silences, or its ebullient upheaval from various critters, he was sitting so comfortably in the chair he could have dozed off. But he feared missing the transformation of day into dark night.

Twisting around slowly, he looked at his uncle and said, in a serious voice, "If we started counting right now, Martin, how long do you think it would take us to count all the stars?"

The sky was spread with stars and planets like a mine strike of golden-studded walls. He could imagine the scream of the miner finding the golden horde, how it would echo down through tunnels of the earth itself, until it faded away to silence.

O'Keeffe, just as comfortable in his chair, and deeply thankful for the younger man's artistic endeavor, knowing that at another time he could fall asleep, looked up and said, "No matter how long it would take on this side, Morgan, we'd only be able finish on the other side. I think there's that many up there and we don't have that much time."

And even as he spoke, this was the time of day that the little blonde girl squeezed into the hollow tree, the one with the blue eyes and the golden hair, came back to erupt his day, throw all the good parts of it into the mix with all the bad parts, this special part that came back as the ultimate slam on his soul. He imagined, as he did so many times, that he could have been a notorious bank robber or held up stagecoaches or railroad trains or freighters and had his picture or poster spread across the land, and never felt this badly. A posse could have chased him across the grass for miles or into the hills and canyons and rocky passes where men were killed at the snap of a finger. He knew all of that. It probably was a whisker away from him his whole life, from that fateful moment when he looked into her eyes. He tried to find the message in it, knowing that the comfort of his bed would not hold off what was coming at him as it did every night.

Carter, eyeing his uncle as he always did, knowing what was on his mind, what came at him on noisy nights, could not begin to guess the truth of the matter, as his uncle said, as he did every night, "Well, I guess I better hit the sack and get ready for tomorrow."

This night, former Sergeant Martin O'Keeffe, emigrant from the wars of Ireland, veteran of the Great War between the States, survivor of innumerable Indian campaigns, escapee from wars of his own making, had no idea what morning held in store for him.

The drums had beat, the word had flown, the answer had come back on the breath of air itself; and so it was, on the morning following, that she was there, astride a great black stallion, the sun at her back like it was fire itself, her golden hair more golden than ever thought possible, strands of it like strings of gold caught in a breeze, and sitting the saddle of the black as if she had been born onto it.

Carter, sound sleeper most times, had slept peacefully this night, and woke early. His first look at the day brought her vision into his eyes. Without surprise he was enamored of her.

He woke his uncle from the deepest sleep he had seen the man have in months, his hand touching O'Keeffe lightly on the shoulder.

"You have a visitor," he said, without having spoken once to the stranger sitting a saddle like a queen might sit a saddle. "You have a visitor, Uncle Martin, a beautiful blonde who has not yet said a word."

In pants and shirt hastily donned, moccasins on his feet, Martin O'Keeffe went to meet his visitor. One look into her eyes, at the spread of her golden hair, an aura in place, he knew who she was.

"You are Sergeant O'Keeffe?" she said, her voice the voice of a queen, authority in place.

"Yes," he said, "I am."

"Sergeant O'Keeffe from River Hill?"

"Sorry to say, yes I am."

"You know me now?" There was a slight turn in her voice, a minor hesitation, a softening.

"I have seen you every day of your life since then, without fail."

"You saved my life. You gave me the life of the Lakota Sioux. You I have not forgotten either." She turned in the saddle as an old Indian stepped out of the barn.

"You are Lakota," she said, with no question in her tone.

"I am Three Bears. Here they call me Sioux Said So. You come from River Hill. I have seen you before, in the tepee of Broken Hand."

"He was my Sioux father, since River Hill, and this man, O'Keeffe, saved my life. He is forgiven his errors and is honored in my tepee for all time."

Morgan Carter, afraid that she'd turn around and leave, stepped down off the porch. "Will you have breakfast with us? Is your name Betty?" He did not know what else to say.

At the barn, the other Indians stepped into the sunlight.

"I am Lakota Betty. Betty is the only thing I remember from my other life, before O'Keeffe saved me, a voice calling my name. Betty, she said, a woman, my mother I think."

She looked at the Indians and said, "We all eat together?"

"Yes," Carter said, "here we all eat together, every day."

Lakota Betty looked at O'Keeffe and said, "You have come a long journey. A very long journey." She nodded in an imperial way and added, "I will eat with all of you."

She smiled at Carter who took the reins from her hand, and felt the exchange deep inside.

And Martin O'Keeffe, as he'd say for days coming, felt the earth shake as Lakota Betty stepped down on his small piece of Earth.

14

Puma-Dog, heavily burdened yet bound in belief, wondered about the inside of the mountain he was climbing, and the trail so old in the making that he could not begin to measure its age. Even the old chief and man of wisdom, One-Wing-Gone, told him the mountain was as old as the gods themselves. "They came as one before they became many," he explained to Puma-Dog on the 13th celebration of all his moons. "One becomes many, to serve, to light the path, to push against darkness, to fill tribal history with heroes all going back to where they came from, from the Heart-of-the-Mountain, and to be served.

Puma-Dog kept remembering One-Wing-Gone repeating one stern piece of advice, "Bury your heroes in the Heart-of-the-Mountain, in the Caves-of-the-Gods." He knew he would hear the words forever, following him in every action beside his brothers.

"How do we find the Caves-of-the-Gods?" Puma-Dog asked, in the 15th Journey of His Moon, a brave full of curiosity, wonder, and holder of the long stories he had remembered from the Hearts of Fires, the fires where the elders related the history of the tribe.

"There is no map, no marked trail, no signs to follow," One-Wing-Gone had replied, "but a close look into one's great heart will find the Heart-of-the-Mountain. It is the law of the gods and the law of the mountain."

Puma-Dog remembered his young excitement when he asked One-Wing-Gone if he had ever been to the Caves-of-the-Gods.

"Of course," One-Wing-Gone replied, "many times. It is where I buried my hero brothers, those fallen in battle, and those who knew I would bring them to the final honor."

"Many times? You lost many brothers?" He could not picture One-Wing-Gone losing a battle, an elder with a face like a hatchet sharpened for war, with eyes as keen as the eagle's on the edge of a wind and sitting in the air above the mountain itself and above all their enemies.

But it was One-Wing-Gone who marveled at the young brave who never knew he'd been touched by the gods in such a special way that he would not only find the Caves-of-the-Gods but would reside there forever when his turn came.

Those to whom he told Puma-Dog's story were sworn to

secrecy, never to tell another soul what they had heard or their places in the Heart-of-the-Mountain would be given away to others.

One-Wing-Gone would tell the story like this: "When he was a boy, not yet named with his true name, he was hunting a puma in the mountains with his dog, Star. He and Star were brothers and had been many places together, and they had tracked the puma, the father of all pumas, onto the level just below the peak of the mountain, where you could first hear the mountain's heartbeat with your ear placed close to the wall of rock. Rains came swiftly from the outlands and from new black clouds, which promised to wipe away all traces of the puma. The two hunters had no idea where the puma was exactly when the storm hit and the skies were suddenly laden with lightning and thunder of the greatest order, and darkness itself came and went in turns with the lightning. In the middle of the storm, lightning kept flashing into other valleys and canyons and behind other peaks as if war itself was being waged in the heavens and thrown by a giant god's hand onto the earth.

"In one majestic flash of lightning brighter than a huge forest fire, a bolt flew from the hand of the god and struck right beside the boy and Star. The boy never felt the touch of the bolt, and to this day does not remember it coming so close. But when he came to, when his young senses returned to him, he woke up flat on the ground. Slowly he opened his eyes and looked directly into the eyes of Star who was dead but wide-eyed beside him. Sadness struck at the boy who loved his dog, even as Star's eyes were staring in awe as if looking at something he had never seen, something beyond both of them.

"When the boy turned to look where he thought Star was staring, the puma was there with his mouth open and teeth as sharp as arrow heads filling that mouth. The puma's eyes were staring at Star as if that was the last sight his eyes would ever see.

"At that moment, not knowing what he had been through, he took his name as 'Puma-Dog,' a tribute to both animals."

One-Wing-Gone would say, with each telling of the story, "The Gods told me the story of Puma-Dog, one even he does not know, for he must earn his way into the Caves-of-the-Gods, which, strange as it seems, has been his fate all along. But you are sworn from this moment never to tell this story to another inside or outside the tribe, even beside one of the Hearts of Fire. The gods will attend you and your silence."

We come back to Puma-Dog, heavily burdened yet bound in belief, wondering about the Heart-of-the-Mountain, and the Caves-of-the-Gods. For the last day and a half he had labored with the great weight on his back, the weight of a great warrior, a great friend, Only-Deer-Leg, who had measured and taken down more than a dozen warriors in the battle with the Comanche enemy, and who had finally taken a spear at Puma-Dog's back, saving his life.

When the enemy's fight disintegrated and they finally disappeared from the canyon, and all Puma-Dog's companions had departed, leaving Puma-Dog with the responsibility, and the promise, of getting Only-Deer-Leg to his proper burial place, in the Heart-of-the-Mountain, in the Caves-of-the-Gods. By turn, he found his hero's quiver, some of his arrows, his great spear and stone club, all sharing Comanche blood. From the last encampment he found a deerskin blanket belonging to Only-Deer-Leg, a string of bear claws, and three scalps prominently displayed on a pole. He wrapped all the prizes of his friend and hero in the blanket and set off for the Caves-of-the-Gods in the Heart-of-the-Mountain, mounted on a horse found wandering in the canyon of the battle. Puma-Dog thought it fitting that the animal was a Comanche pony.

At a ledge of the mountain, where the trail was no longer passable for the horse, Puma-Dog started carrying all the parts of Only-Deer-Leg. The load was as heavy as the onus of his delivery to the sacred place. He kept talking to his friend: "We will find our way in to the Heart–of-the-Mountain, I promise." Puma-Dog also felt the weight of that promise, which sat on his shoulders like the world itself.

At various times he had to put down one or the other of his load, the body of Only-Deer-Leg or his war prizes, all the parts of a warrior's life bound for eternity. One part of the load would be left in a secure place, while the other was lugged onward to another selected place on his route to the mountain. When it was the body of Only-Deer-Leg to be left, it had to be protected from creatures of the mountain and creatures of the sky, to whom the gods had given the right to feast on all remains found on the face of the earth.

Places where covering rocks and boulders were scarce, he had to find a shelter in among the rocks, such as a small cave or indentation or an overhang that would serve his need of protecting the last remains of Only-Deer-Leg.

Puma-Dog kept talking to his friend: "The Caves-of-the-Gods

are in front of us, not behind us. We are getting close to your forever sleeping place. I do not know the path or the true trail, but it is in front of us. I can swear to that with all my heart, which tells me I am going the right way."

Once, as he struggled with his load, he saw in the distance, on another part of the mountain, a brave struggling under another load, and knew that warrior was lost. He felt badly for the brave who was carrying his own burden. It made Puma-Dog think about his confidence in finding a resting place for Only-Deer-Leg, but his resolve did not waver at the sight of the other burdened warrior. Only new bursts of energy and hope sprang up in him.

Once more, a strange thought hit him, thinking he had heard an eagle say, "Just follow me when you have a doubt. You and I have shared the sky and all that has been in it from the beginning."

Puma-Dog did not know what that message meant, having no idea that an eagle could know lightning first hand from the same sky the way Puma-Dog knew it, or One-Wing-Gone, or those who had been told the story beside the Hearts-of-Fire. But he kept looking up at the great sky, seeking the spread of wings above him, seeking the eagle whose voice he had heard saying words he did not understand … but words he would trust if he ever understood them.

Nature, or parts of nature, he believed, had always sent him these secret messages. They could be truth from the highest order, but he did not know that, nor if things accepted became what they were meant to be.

A second creature of the earth spoke to him in another surprise; it was the voice of the dead puma who shared his name; "Even as you doubt my voice now, and doubt me, I know more than you. I know all about you. If you can find me this time, I will be in the Cave of the Gods, in the Heart of the Mountain and will tell you all there is to know, all you ever wanted to know."

At that moment, from the fair and clear sky above them, a bolt of lightning hit the mountain and through a sudden opening Puma-Dog saw the holy ground and carried Only-Deer-Leg and all his treasures into the Heart of the Mountain, and as Puma-Dog set down his friend and hero, he himself fell dead in the spot long ago reserved for him, and he instantly knew all things the puma had promised.

Cowboy Dawn

He rolled over in his blanket and watched the false dawn migrate from behind the mountains. A sense of peace prevailed about him, the last sound a distant coyote selling his wares, or claiming them, being part of dawn's celebration, as his sleepy self was. The single howl settled into a canyon and was lost forever; had run its course this time out. In the shadows the hills were still locked into, shapes and shadows of no description but which everything fit into including the steep hills he'd have to climb before the day was done, life was bent on moving at its pace. He was at peace with that, as though it might be a compromise on what was coming his way; as if he'd take whatever was coming along.

He was not hunted. He was not hunting.

He was waiting.

From under the cover of the blanket he withdrew his boots, covered for the night, warm beside his legs instead of on them. Tethered to a bush, his horse nickered, acknowledging him and the coming drink and the romp on the grass. A star was brightly visible in the western sky, out of a steep reach of the Teton Range; it was a grand hello for the day, from the day.

He put all the parts together; pre-dawn, horse, coyote, the smell of the grass and the odor of a dead fire that would soon come back in coffee's breakthrough, the squeeze of boots settling their wrap about his feet and ankles, the sure touch of stirrups as if welded in place, his rump promising the horse's bounce and run.

The new day.

The new hope.

The horse, as golden as the sun would promise the day, tossed about a rich palomino's mane that'd dance in the wind before the day was an hour old, the mane like a golden fleece. That dance would be a renewal, he believed, as he tried to think back to more than two weeks earlier. The memory of the time was dim, shaded or shielded, still caught up as parts of the old day and the old shadows, the old shapes of what was, what is, what had become.

The ledge trail was narrow, tricky at times, but he'd made the trip a half dozen times without one incident. The cave, its mouth as narrow as pursed lips, had been there for a few thousand years, he surmised. He'd never paid much attention to it, other than agreeing that it was there in stone, a slight slit in the stone face. The river was there, too, a precipitous 300 feet down the palisaded side of the mountain, sheerer than a chance at a Royal Straight Flush, a pot looming in the middle of a table, all hands at work.

"Never look down," McKusker had told him before the start of his first trip. "I been there a hundred times, kid, and I never looked down and I never fell. The trip saves you a half day, rather than run around the mountain. That's one whole day saved for town. Special is what it is."

McKusker was an old hand at the Double Star Ranch. Some said he was there longer than the owner, had lost it to him in a poker game. Life, many of the hands agreed, could turn on the flip of a coin, a single draw from the deck, an errant shot awing on chance, a dead trigger when you really needed one more shot, a look a girl might have thrown your way once and you had a speck of dust in your eye and never saw the message she had sent your way.

A thousand chance things could happen one at a time.

But McKusker never had a cougar scream at him, at his horse, on the narrowest part of the ledge, from where that slit cave mouth was. McKusker never went off a saddle as the horse reared, slipped, fell away like a side of the mountain itself, like a damned landslide or a chunk of cliff sheared off by an earthquake in the heart of the mountain. Down. Going down. All the way down.

He had lost his ranch in a corner of a saloon, at a table of chance, the crowd squeezing in on him.

The fall of the horse, off the ledge, made him shiver again.

The incident flashed back to him in pieces. "Don't fall under the horse," he had told himself as he too fell away, in air, in space, in the once pale gray day with his horse. "You'll fall safely into the water, and then the damned horse will fall right on top of you and kill you forever."

He felt like he was swimming in the gray air, waving and wagging his arms, sending signals, praying for help, wondering where the horse was. His hat was gone. His side arms. The canteen sounded tinny as it hit the back of his head. He'd have no need of water anyway. He caught no laughter on his part. He thought about the horse in a flash; would the horse survive? Had the cougar, so close, nearly into the grip of the stirrups, scared the horse to death? Would he be dead, the horse, before he hit the river? He remembered the expression being said a dozen times in different stories in the bunkhouse; "He was dead before he hit the ground." Would it be the same with water? With a horse?

He couldn't hear the river as he fell, not the way it always sounded, a roar as steady as wind in the tunnels of the mountain, never letting go as the temperature fluctuations changed the rush of air into sounds full of mystery, of unknown sources, as constant as day start.

In part of the fall he wondered how many had fallen from this ledge in a thousand years. How many cowboys on the way to town? How many Indians, in a sudden storm, lightning coming down on top of them, the mountain shaking as Mother Nature made another pass at some small, indeterminate life on the move? As she drew on fate?

Finally, he did not remember hitting the water. No pain. No slam. No submersion in the midst of a new wilderness he had never known, the clutch of water, the iron grip of it deep in the body of it. Or being drawn out of the river a half mile or more down past the rapids and falls he had gone through, upside down, inside out, head or feet first, obviously not conscious, for none of it had come back, none of it would come back. Should he try to bring it back? he thought seriously. A part of his life gone forever, as simple as that last coyote's howl went away down in a canyon, lost.

The old Indian, the one who pulled him out of the water, who saw him fall, who saw his horse fall and knew the horse would not survive, who knew the man had a chance if he carried enough air in his lungs. The Indian said he did not jump into the water to save him because he was too old, but snagged him with a long stick, dragged him close to the bank, then pulled him up from the reach of water to lie on the ground, to find one breath that brought him back.

"One breath. It was close," he said, nodding as serene as the mountain, being spokesman for the mountain.

His name was Buffalo-Die-Hard, an elder, a shaman of the Blackfeet nation, older than some of the trees that swayed in the breeze around him, yet strong enough to haul him up on the bank of the river, once he had floated past the wildest part of the rapids and the falls, barely alive.

"You come to me from the God of the Mountain and the God of the River," Buffalo-Die-Hard had said when he came conscious. They promised me, as old as I am, a chance to save a life and you are indebted to me forever. But you are on the short side to owe me."

21

There was humor in his few words, a twinkle in his eyes, the way one owes up to a mystery, and then lets it go as a judgment is concluded.

That's when Buffalo-Die-Hard drew everything into focus. "The cougar was born of the two gods to do their bidding. The cougar use his roar to drive the horse to his death and leave you for me. Tell me why you use this trail alone. Why do you not go with others around the mountain? Other Blackfeet, younger, much younger, find life different, seek excitement, danger. They try to measure man out there? They only will know what I know when they come to this edge of a long life."

"I go to visit a woman who will become my wife."

"Does she agree with that?"

"She doesn't know it yet."

The twinkle came back to the eyes of Buffalo-Die-Hard. "Does she wait for you now? Does she know you are late to see her?"

"I'll tell her when the time comes," he replied to the old Indian, as good as he could make on a promise, and he meant it. "It was my turn to go to town. They will miss me, at some ranch, even if she doesn't. But I'll tell her everything when the time comes."

"Will you tell her about Buffalo-Die-Hard? How the God of the Mountain and the God of the River told me about you?"

"Yes," he said to the wise one, "I will tell her all that I remember when the time comes."

"What is my name?"

"Buffalo-Die-Hard. You are a Blackfoot Indian, a shaman or wise man."

"Yes, I am a wise man. I know my own name as well as you know my name Buffalo-Die-Hard. You can tell her that." The eyes were speaking again before his tongue. "What is your name?" He laughed. "You think Indian has no laugh in him? You think Buffalo-Die-Hard has no humor like white man has, man who does not know his own name. Will you tell her when the time come?"

"Tell her what?"

"Tell her what your name is."

"When I remember it, when the time comes, when she promises to marry me."

"What will her name be then?"

"I don't know. Not now, but it will come back to me. I can feel it coming back. I'm scratching for it. I lost my horse and I'll never get

22

him back. But my name's right there someplace."

"When it come, tell me who you are, what is your name, so I will know whose life belong to me."

"My name is Larry Pumphrey." It was the first name that came to him. Larry was an old pard. He had not seen him in years. He wondered what had happened to good old Larry. What did Larry call him?

"If her name is to become Pumphrey," Buffalo-Die-Hard said, "you are in trouble with her. She would be named Lady-with-Husband-with-No-Name."

He had been waiting for so long he had forgotten how long, but, as if a miracle had come upon him, he said, "My name is Clifford George Cagney. I am a drover at the Double-Star Ranch."

The old Blackfoot Indian said, "All of Cagney owe life to Buffalo-Die-Hard, until lady say different. Then all Cagney owe the lady."

Crescent Moon for One-Dog-Left

The Indian papoose was found tucked between two rocks in a copse of cottonwoods and pines in the Utah/Idaho territory by a mountain man, Tall Lennie, so named by Indians of the area, who was following a deer he had shot. He found that a wounded dog had fallen at the baby's side, which from the signs he read told him the dog had been badly hurt in a fight protecting the child and possibly had run off whatever creature was too close. But two other dogs were torn to pieces. Not far away a dead Indian pony had been scavenged by the same fierce creature and perhaps by vultures also.

The scene, in some manner, was re-created in Tall Lennie's mind, and nothing would ever change it. The papoose was lost and protected by dogs of the tribe, the mother might be dead somewhere, or chased off or carried off if she had hid her papoose from harm.

The moon made the time exact for Tall Lennie. A few days after the new moon, the waxing crescent moon appeared in the western horizon soon after sunset. That was the night the baby was found. Two weeks later, to the day, the full moon would rise in the east and be visible all during the night, to set in the west near sunrise. It was like a clock of days in Tall Lennie's head. He'd mark the Indian baby forever by the moon and its time, though he could not tell to which tribe the papoose belonged. It made a great difference to him where the child should be brought for caring.

Tall Lennie, named by some Shoshones with whom he traded, picked up the child, named him One-Dog-Left the way his mother might have, and headed for the Webster settlement on the big river, where the baby could be cared for. One couple he knew without a child of their own seemed the most adaptable to taking in the baby, and the most welcome. He had sat a few times at the Vickers' table when the talk came up about no children in the house. Martha Vickers was comely, adjusted, and hardworking, the western life suiting her appetite for life, but she wanted a child. Her sister had been carried off by Indians five years earlier, on her way to visit Martha and her husband Jon. She too had been childless. The void in Martha Vickers' life had been filled by her energy.

Now that void had found a new cause for directing energy ... and love. In one momentous swing of time, chance and good fortune, her life changed when the baby napped for a while in her arms. Her husband eventually made dinner for Tall Lennie, as his wife fed the infant and moved things about the house so quickly that Tall Lennie's head began to spin.

"She move this fast usual?" Tall Lennie said to Jon Vickers.

"When she's a mind, Lennie, which is usual, as you say. Plumb glad you thought about her and me and not some that would've turned their nose up at an Indian papoose." The two men had a mutual liking for the other, both of them different in the way of life, the difference acceptable to the other.

"Seems like I ain't seen that kind of happy since old Jack Mellon found his daughter in Ogden just walkin' down the street in front of him. Caused a happy ruckus they did and Jack near got to huggin' me, if you can believe that, and him not seein' her for most five years."

"You know Martha'll protect that child with her life from this moment on, like the good Lord left him in her care, with your help of course."

"I don't know that He touched me, Jon, but He sure touched that papoose and Martha too. They's like poison ivy and white skin getting' locked up come spring in the air."

"Tell me again about the name you gave him, Lennie. It come on you quick?"

"Like this, Jon," he said while snapping his fingers in the air, "with the dog passin' like he did and me holdin' him and the babe at the same time, and I spilt some water on him by accident and called his name right out like I was Injun myself right in their tribe."

"Then you can be sure, Lennie," said Martha from the other room, "that we'll call him by his blessed name and won't ever try to hide he's Indian from him. Not on this ranch. Not in this house. Not by his new parents. Not ever."

Tall Lennie knew he had brought One-Dog-Left to the right place.

The boy, not without some concern on the part of the Vickers about his relationship with others in the settlement, grew apace of his years. He was adept at all duties and implements of a cowman, from horse and cow to rope and weapon. He showed skill and courage many times over, and was elated whenever Tall Lennie came to visit, usually once a year, now and then twice on special occasions. One of them being the birth date Tall Lennie had settled on the boy from the best he could figure. Once he told Martha and Jon about the moon on the night of discovering the boy was the first quarter of the crescent moon, in the month of June. That determined the date of birth in his mind.

One-Dog-Left was fifteen years old on the second year that Tall Lennie failed to show up. It was June 6, 1876, his birthday, and he sat on the corral fence most of the day, gazing off to the foothills and the range beyond, expecting to see Tall Lennie, like a tree shorn of all branches but one, come riding out of the foothills the way he had so many times, slim, ramrod straight, a hearty wave of one arm that made him look like he was 10 foot tall in the saddle and his horse a miniature pony.

He had not eaten since breakfast, skipping two meals as he sat, near motionless for hours at a time on the rail. Martha watched him from her kitchen window, knowing what was in his mind, what the urges were that passed into him, deep into him, for resolution. She had been there many times herself, knowing the drive that kept her alive, the hope for a child, for her lost sister, for the goodness that one might have in this life.

Not once during the day did she call him for a meal.

When he did move off the rail, near dusk, she knew he had made a decision whose effect he would carry all his life.

One-Dog-Left entered the barn where Jon Vickers worked with two ranch hands. "Pa," One-Dog-Left said, "I'm going to look for Uncle Lennie in the morning. I'm going alone. I don't know how long I'll be gone or what I will find. I'm going in to tell Mom now." He turned and left the barn, a decided adult stride in his walk, a man's stride. Jon Vickers remembered the day he had come to them in the arms of the man he'd now go looking for. To a certain degree, he understood the swirl of life about them all.

"Mom," One-Dog-Left said to Martha Vickers, "I'm going out in the morning to look for Uncle Lennie. It's been too long this time. I don't know where I'll go or what I'll find, or even how long I'll be, but I'll be back." He hugged her and sat down to eat a late meal she had ready in minutes.

Silently, without motion, she watched him from the other room, the love still shooting through her, the pride she had taken in raising him, all the while knowing that someday something in him would call him elsewhere. She had talked to other women who had lost their children, not to war or strife or a life of crime or sitting a sheriff's saddle, but of a choice that rose in the spirit of the person, a choice that demanded or looked for answers, opportunities, or new love. None of them ever fully understood the loss. It was at this moment that Martha Vickers knew hers so completely.

Before dawn, before the rooster sounded his alarm or the guinea hens in the tree tops were squawking at false dawn's gray entrance, One-Dog-Left was away from the ranch, and no one behind him risen yet, though Martha Vickers knew he was gone. The emptiness filled her as she wondered when, if ever, she'd see her son again.

In the Uinta Mountains, two days ride from the Green River, he found an old Shoshone Indian who gave him the first news about Tall Lennie. "Man ride high in saddle. Saw him one time, six moons ago, with Black Quiver. Leg broke. Get carried away by squaws to Black Quiver lodge up there." He pointed deeper and higher in the mountains. "His horse dead from bear. Stay all winter in mountain place. But not there now. One Wing tell me he is in a new place in mountains. Has new Indian wife, but no Shoshone."

One- Dog-Left said, "I will go look for him. Thank you."

"Are you the papoose he find years ago, mother dead from bear also? Tall man take you to white ranch. Are you that Shoshone papoose, now try to find tall man?"

"That is who I am."

"If you find tall man, you can take new name. You can pick any name. You can think about it long time if you find tall man. He tell story about you all the time in the mountains. Shoshone never bother him. Never take game from his trap. Never steal his horse. Fix broke leg so he can get new woman."

The old Indian looked into the boy's eyes. "I see big battle coming. Big chiefs fight past mountains. Woman fights with her husband, saves life of brother name Chief Comes-in-Sight, but she will fall down from sickness. Woman is not tall man's woman, but a Cheyenne woman. Woman make man many ways. Strong is one way. Cook meat is another. Carry arrows another. Chief Washakie, with his woman, white woman, make war on Blackfeet, Cheyenne and Sioux. He has room in heart for tall man who save Shoshone papoose. He will know you in the mountains."

One-Dog-Left rode north, climbed trails, dipped into valleys and canyons, followed what came to him as Shoshone trails. The signs appeared to him as if he had seen them all his life … where a summer tipi had been set up, lived in, taken down … where game had been dressed down from a kill, treated, or cooked over an open fire, where a night guard had lain for hours on the watch for tribal enemies or army scouts, where a dance had taken place on the long grass. The unknown chants came to him the way they would in a dream.

Uncle Lennie had spoken of all such things on every visit, as if he knew the day would come when One-Dog-Left would need such knowledge.

The time was here. It was happening, and the boy who'd become a man thought often of the man that brought him to a new home, from out of the desperate wilds, his mother dead, her horse dead, the dogs gone in their last fight. He wondered what the dogs had been called. Dog-Stand-On-Two-Legs sounded as good as any name he thought of.

From one point, as high as he had been in the mountains, and from a distance, he saw several Indians, hours apart, walk up to and disappear as if a wall of rock had swallowed them whole. He marked the wall in several ways so that he could see it from other points, and eventually look directly down on the place where the Indians seemed to disappear … though he knew it was into the mountain somehow. Uncle Lennie had told him of the many places where man and animal lived out the harsh winters … with water available, a cache of firewood set aside for cooking and warmth, food, fur or skins for comfort, and means to replenish the food supply.

And all the time he suddenly realized that when Uncle Lennie seemed to be telling the most thrilling stories, he was telling him how he himself had survived in the wild mountains, or how it might be done.

He was glad he had listened to the man of the mountains. Now he hoped he could find him, and alive.

A day later, from another lookout point, he spotted the entrance into the mountain. It had to be behind a huge sheaf of rock that had peeled off the face of the cliff.

The next evening, as dusk settled in, he entered a virtual hole in the mountain and made his way along a tunnel without light to a turn in the tunnel. As he made that turn he saw a sliver of light ahead of him, smelled the odor of burning pitch and heard voices.

One voice said, "Tall man must get boy to come here. He is son of chief and must be told of his place. Tall man owe life to us. We bring you here, fix leg, feed you all this time. Must get boy to come here."

One-Dog-Left heard Uncle Lennie say, "And you kept me a prisoner all the time. I could have gone out of here many moons ago. If I tell One-Dog-Left how this saving man has been treated, he will burn your villages, bring the devil himself into the heart of the mountain, put the curse of the fire god on all the Shoshones."

"But he is Shoshone too," the Indian voice said.

"He is fair before he is Shoshone. The God of all things and all ways is in his blood before the Shoshone blood. You know that and so do I. His true mother is sister of his ranch mother. When he finds that out he will bring fire on you, perhaps a new war. He is son of Chief Washakie and will be a chief of the Shoshones of the Nations."

"He must learn our ways all the way before he becomes a chief of Shoshone. We all agree new chief must learn our ways." There was a rumbling of voices that seemed to go the length of the tunnel before it came back in an echo, many voices in the echo.

"Hah," Tall Lennie said, "all of you know he is as much Shoshone now as you are. He knows all the ways of the Shoshone. Even now he knows I am in trouble and will come for me. That is his way, the true Shoshone way. I know it has been told to you. One-Dog-Left is a Shoshone chief without knowing it."

One-Dog-Left was stunned in his place, in the darkness of a tunnel in the heart of a mountain. As he envisioned his ranch mother, he saw a dark spirit of a woman enter the picture in his mind. He could not remember her, but he knew her. He could feel his true mother in his blood. There was such a war now breeding in his blood … he was part Shoshone, son of Chief Washakie, and he was part white, as well as a real part of the ranch of the Vickers.

His eyes, sitting so long in the darkness, began to see things around him. He saw a stack of firewood along one wall of the tunnel. A pile of fur stood as high as his hips on the other side of the tunnel. The flicker of a small flame appeared, and smoke swirled upward from the flame, to escape through a hole in the mountain, he believed. No stench of old fire or old cooking came to him, and the swirl of smoke from the fire continued to rise and escape in some overhead manner.

A sense of power began to flow in his blood as he stood there, listening to his past, hearing his future. The power began to mobilize itself, become a conscious part of his thinking. What would a Shoshone chief do now?

The power came upon him with great convincing, the way a weight is known on the shoulders. It pushed itself through his body, into his mind.

The Shoshone spirit ran right up his backside. "Hold there," he yelled out, in a voice that rang off the rock walls and ran into all the mountainous cavities. He took a new name on the spot and declared it. "Chief Ten-Dogs-Ready comes to speak to all who must listen. The tall man is my friend. He will walk from here as he chooses. No Shoshone will bother him. Chief Ten-Dogs-Ready has made a new law for all Shoshones of his lodge."

The echo of that voice, its power, ran back and forth in the tunnel and into the other passageways, the whole mountain ringing with the truth from the tongue of a new Shoshone chief.

Tall Lennie, noting who the newcomer was, said his piece also. "Did not I tell you that the new chief would look for me? Now he is here and we will leave this heart of the mountain. He has come as I said and not as you wished him to come. Chief Ten-Dogs-Ready, son of Chief Washakie already with long tooth, and a woman of the ranch, will do as he wishes, will wear the hat or dressed feathers of his choice, ride his own horse, live in the world as he chooses. His lodge will be the lodge he makes, wherever he puts down the poles to hold the skins against the weather."

The two men, each having rescued the other from peril or pain, from chance or choice, made their way down the tunnel to the entrance to the mountain. No Indian challenged their leaving the heart of the mountain, the mountain range, or the way down to the wide prairie.

Martha Vickers, from her kitchen window, saw them first, the tall, thin man in the saddle waving a thin arm in the air, and the younger one, easily known, riding comfortably on an Indian pony, wearing no shirt but wearing a hawk's feather in his hair, also waving his arms, each man knowing that the lady of the ranch house was looking for them all the time they were gone.

Tall Lennie died from a fall off a ledge in the Uinta Mountains in May of 1879. He had no known kin except the Shoshone chief, of an eastern tribe and of the widespread Vickers ranch, who would be known, eventually, as Chief Father-of-Three-Vickers-Boys, who died in 1938, killed by a bear in the Uinta Mountains near a copse of cottonwoods and pine trees. When two Shoshone braves found him, a dog, taking last breaths, was at his side, and his horse was a short ways off, being fed upon by the vultures. They found bear tracks in the copse.

In all the lodges his story is told, about One-Dog Left and Ten-Dogs-Ready. The rest is understood as that which might not have happened.

The Legend of Blue Soldier Riding, Kiowa

The High Chief of Clouds, he was sure, had sent the landslide, and vengeance was left to him and him alone. All the others were gone. Gray Dove was gone. One Wing was gone. Puma Path was gone. His best friend Eagle Claw and all the others were gone. For his own life, he said his thank you to The High Chief of Clouds, "Aahóow" it was said. In a soft chant deep in the cave, he sang his thanks repeatedly. But when he tried to chant "in the language" the names of those he had lost in the raid, they jumped around like hummingbirds and caught in his throat, threatening to choke him. "I will die with a hard memory," sounded in his head, but strong Kiowa vengeance tossed it away like a feather from a nest, no more to be remembered. After all, he was Kiowa, fierce, relentless, warrior of the plains, horseman without match. His blood, he knew, would long sing the names.

Before all this was over, he would take himself to Bear Butte far in the north, the sacred place, "K'ówp·éytto" it was called and it would be good for him and all the others. He would lift their names to The High Chief of the Clouds and Dead River himself would come back to a good life when he offered up his name, "Pééy p'óó." All would be blessed again; many drawings on the robes of the elders said it was so, robes where events were marked and time kept in its place and where the promises coming almost became visible.

The landslide had saved his life, coming down between him and the pursuing troop of soldiers who had destroyed his village. With the onus of vengeance on him, he accepted the loss of all his implements. In his scramble for safety, the clutter of rocks and debris had taken possession of his horse, bow, arrows, quiver, his only knife, and even the blanket Gray Dove had made for him. The only things keeping him warm in the cave he had found were the pine boughs he dragged in behind him during the night, through the solid mass of devil's claw hiding the entrance. No trooper would follow him; off horseback they were lost, and he knew it as well as they did. This was Indian country, along the Rio Grande Valley, up from the jungles south of there, down from the ice bridges in the north, past "K'ówp·éytto" sitting so proudly on Mother Earth as if the High Chief had set it in place so all would think of him.

It was only three days since he had started alone out on his hunt, as Good Chief had requested. His real name day was coming where he would meet up with himself, as Good Chief had said. "You will find your real name on this hunt. Be aware." Now Good Chief would not know he had taken the name of "Blue Soldier Riding." Would he understand when the name became known? Would there be shame? Would other braves make fun of his name, even if he was Kiowa? Does anybody make fun of a Kiowa name?

He reflected back on the start of his trek, saying goodbye to Gray Dove at the edge of the teepee village. Before he knew it, the great river was in front of him. With some planning and good fortune the river crossing had gone well, his horse Wolf Boy, "Kûy thalíi," strong enough to fight the surge of water that came out of the canyon wall in a quick rush, as if long rains had been chasing him for days on end. He wondered about the name "Long Rain," but had not seen the long rain, so that name was put aside. "Great Fish" did not come or "Hawk on Ledge" or "Puma Plunge." For two full days he was nameless.

And then, at a sharp turn in the mountainside trail, he saw great smoke rising as he came back toward his village, where three days earlier 100 teepees had spread across the plains like sunshine. Then, like a hawk had dropped it across his path in the path of the wind, he smelled fire, and the burning of flesh, a disgusting odor coming upon him.

Still astride the main trail on The Big Mountain, he suddenly became aware that some riders were nearby. Horse smell came first to him and then he saw the soldier in blue on the top of a rest, motioning to others that he had probably seen a lone Indian on the trail. One soldier caused him no fear, but he did not know how many others were behind him, back down the trail on the other side of the mountain.

It would be best to find out how many dared pursue him. He whipped Wolf Boy into a fast run back on the trail. The lone rider in blue followed him, a good rider on a good horse, he determined in a few quick looks. A strong horse, a big red horse, moved like a prairie fire in the wind, a horse as good as Wolf Boy, and he was gaining on him.

Then the gods interfered, The Mountain God and the High Chief, as a loud crack, as loud as the voice of an angry Thunder God spoke, and the Good Earth God shook all over, and part of the mountain came down on the two riders. Everything growing in the path of the landslide came down, pinon trees, devil's claw with its thick, coarse hairs on long leaves, manzanita he knew as bearberry shrub with red bark and oval-shaped leaves, tall pine trees torn by awesome power from deep-dowsing roots gone down to unknown depths.

In that massive movement of earth mix, he thought the last thing in the world he would see was the blue soldier riding on the big horse getting caught up in the overwhelming rush of rocks and unearthed trees. That would become his name if he lived, Blue Soldier Riding. The pain that must have come upon the other rider came upon him as the rush of mountain pushed itself upon him. Wolf Boy's front legs were broken in one swift crush of rock and stone. There was no sound except a collapse of breath escaping the great chest.

Noise surrounded him. Dust entered his eyes. Sat on his tongue. Rocks bounced their chaos around him. Unhorsed, stripped of his gear, he found himself flush against the mountain. A dark opening was beside him and he rolled into it, his hands reaching ahead of him, at search. When they touched the inside wall, he muttered, in the language, "T 'óów ts' óów," cold stone. The white man, the blue soldiers, often used cold stone to mark their graves, but he would not think the cold mountain was going to be his final holy place. After all this, he was still Kiowa.

Hours passed, stars surely passed overhead, and no sounds came from the mountain or from the debris piled up in the bottom of the canyon. And nothing from the blue soldier. No sounds came from his comrades wherever they were or had gone. No search party had made themselves known, as if the blue soldier was already forgotten, discounted, his spirit trying to find its way to wherever such spirits went.

He waited a whole day, thinking of Gray Dove and Eagle Claw and One Wing, and finally believed that they were free and in the wind with all the other birds. And Puma Path would be loose on the Great Mountain, on the scent.

In a bright morning's sun, a hawk cruising on a lift of air rising from the mountain, he crawled out of the cave. The sky was blue as far as he could see, with the exception of one white cloud sitting way off in the western sky like a lost rabbit out on the wide grass. Silence rode the air as if all sound had fled the earth. No wind touched his face where wind was always turning on itself in the heart of canyons, playing games with one's face and mind, like children at play at the edge of the village.

He was hungry. He had no tools, no weapons, but he was Kiowa. He'd go hungry as long as it took him to find food, find a horse, find a way to a friendly village. He was still on his hands and knees when he heard a horse snickering beyond the crush of rocks and uprooted trees. Moving cautiously among the mass of boulders and sheered rock face, the arms and trunks of trees tumbled in a heap at the end of their lives, he stood to get a longer look.

It was amazing; the soldier's horse was there, the great red horse that had pursued him and Wolf Boy, penned in against the face of one cliff, his saddle in place, a canteen still tied to the saddle, a rifle in its long scabbard. Then he saw the blue soldier flat on the floor of the canyon, his head nearly crushed by a stone as big as himself. For the first time he could study a blue soldier, look at his hands, study his wrists and arms, imagine the decisions that had been made by a man now dead, now past all doubts and all decisions. This one looked to have been a strong man, one his own size, but there was no face in which to find a reflection, the way one sees into others as one sees into a placid stream.

Then it hit him; he would soon be known as Blue Soldier Riding. Villages would call his name out. He would wear the soldier's blue clothes, his boots, and his wide-brimmed hat. He would ride his horse and use his weapons. All the world would know of Blue Soldier Riding. Pelts would come to him, beads in great designs from the High Chief himself, a slim girl who could hunt and fish and who might say he could call her Gray Dove if he wanted to.

"Ahye," he said, as he saw a knife sticking from a place in the saddle, a long knife of a kind he had only seen once, in the hands of a great Kiowa who had taken it from a horseman in Mexico, across the wide river. "K'óo" he said under his breath, like it was a prayer, "Knife," it would have said to the soldier if he was listening with an ear for the language.

A patch of food was in a saddle bag. Dry beef jerky, needing good teeth, did its errand. And the horse was given the first water, right from the wide hat. One large rock was moved by using a long limb shorn from a tree. The rock rolled slowly at first, and then rolled a few feet on the canyon floor. Now there was room enough for the horse to leave. The big red drank again from the hat, felt the comfort

35

and the trust in the new hands, and heard the soft whisper in his ear.

Again, confirming he was Kiowa, he was horseman; he agreed with himself that his new horse must have a new name, as he himself had a new name.

For a long while he thought, and then, he touched the horse's neck with a soft pat and a soft voice saying, in the language, "K'óo tséeyñ," Knife Horse. The bonding that had begun long ago on the prairie when the horses came with the Spaniards from below the big river, began anew; a new horse and a new rider, made for each other, and new names for each. He patted the big red once more on the neck, whispered his name in still a softer voice, "K'óo tséeyñ,' thinking it was like talking to Gray Dove out on the soft grass, under the moon laying cover on them.

K'óo tséeyñ answered back.

Studying rifle and knife and the saddle gear, getting his hands comfortable with them, he still yearned for his bow. He'd have to make one, and do that in a hurry. The horse moved easily out of the natural corral, eased his way past more boulders, turned at a reins message, and came out at the end of the landslide. The new weight sat on him evenly and comfortably. At the reach of grass he broke into a spirited run, pulling up in a copse of trees at a new command; where a bow might reside, and arrows might be found.

At a small stream nearby he found enough smelly arrow weed stems to make a dozen arrows. They looked long and true and would fly like the small thief bird. He found and cut wood for a bow, liking the feel of it immediately. Hunger coming at him, a rabbit was snared, a small fire lit at the edge of twilight, the meat cooked quickly, the fire put out, and the animal tethered and watered. He slept a few hours until a distant wolf call, disturbing K'óo tséeyñ, disturbed him. He rose up in the darkness. It was time to go back.

It was time for revenge.

He took a different way back, over another mountain, through numerous valleys, down through a final canyon cutting right into Mother Earth. He came at last to a familiar place, on the side of a mountain that looked down where the village had been, on the meadow where he and Gray Dove had spent a few nights.

The fullness of day was behind him, and when he turned to look back down the trail he had used, he saw two blue soldiers, astride their horses staring at him from a long distance. Without hesitation, the way he had planned it out all in his mind, he crazily shook his rifle over his head, waving them on. They came toward him, dipped around a turn in the trail and disappeared. When they came in sight, around a sharp turn, he dropped one of them with a single arrow. The man fell quickly from his saddle. As the other soldier turned to run or dismount, he fell dead from a rifle shot. A third rider appeared way back down the trail and galloped off.

With speed, the two dead soldiers were stripped of their gear, but not their uniforms, except the yellow patches on their sleeves. He laid them side by side and covered them with a few rocks that scavengers would have trouble moving, and rode off, down into a canyon he knew well.

In the middle of the old village, death still a living sign there, every teepee torn down and burned, but no bodies visible, he drove an arrow into the ground and attached to it the yellow patches he had stripped off the arms of the soldiers, and included those on the shirt he wore.

At the edge of evening he raised his arms to the High Chief of the Clouds who had given him the errand of vengeance. With arms lifted, his very spirit moving from him in thanks, he chanted again and again the words of thanks, "Aahóow," he sang and kept singing, "Aahóow, Aahóow." The echoes of the chant are heard yet, in small canyons, on mountain tops, on the wide prairies under sun and moon and the mix of stars.

The legend has run wild for many years, the legend of Blue Soldier Riding, the Kiowa trying to find again a lost village, and a girl named Gray Dove.

Decision from the Valley of Lost Sun

One of the members of the army patrol, lead scout Sgt. Jacques Emberly, who had rushed far ahead when he heard the first fusillade of gun fire, came over the brow of the trail well before the other troopers would get there and saw the gun flashes and the cloud of rising gun smoke and realized he was looking at a small war. Sounds of rifle fire, repeating in waves, rolled over him, uphill from the circled wagon train on the wide grass, and the smell of the burnt gunpowder assailed his sense of smell as if he had already known the dead lying about and set the statistics for the report he'd have to write. With the smoke from at least a hundred rifles and the constant noise from the wagon train and from the attacking Indians, Pawnee most likely, his mind flew back to Chicago where he grew up, not far from the rail yards and the smell of slaughtered cattle and beef burning on hasty spits not far away where lost and disparaged people scrounged and lived on cast-offs from the endless slaughtering.

How he gotten out of there hit him with a sudden slam, as it always did: he was lucky. It was as simple as that ... he was lucky. He had gotten this far in three enlistments and would soon be due for a fourth decision. It would not be easy this time. He looked back at his luck and it told him so.

Even as he looked at war, at another level of survival, at another cast of luck or chance or karma riding on a black horse or on the cast of the dice, he was lucky.

He reflected on luck and its apparel, its manner of visits. Luck came in disguises, over-dressed or under-dressed, masked or unmasked, on the seat of a saddle or the bare back of an Indian pony, in a sure shot from a slow gun or a lucky shot from a fast gun, in an arrow with someone else's name on it. Luck appeared in all shapes and sizes, and all costumes and rigs, and it often depended on how you looked at it. Don't knock that, he would allow, not any part of it; there were times when luck looked back at you with a scowl, a smile, a face full of ponderous thought or touched with the simplest curiosity.

It likewise said there were choices to be made.

Just like it said his mind would jump around on him, seeing other things, knocking down other ideas and images, going elsewhere in this wild world; luck had control.

He raised his rifle overhead in a hurry-up motion and saw the responding wave from the patrol's guidon bearer. Deciding to find a short haven in the midst of a new war, he made for a single mass of boulders that might have rolled here, in the middle of the prairie, from a high spot, perhaps with the shove of an old-time cataclysmic change from Mother Nature, perhaps the thrust of a glacier as slow as a lost thought coming back from partial oblivion. He thought of time standing still, caught up to itself where it stood in one moment, as if posing to be remembered. Hell, making its own demands.

Draping the horse's reins under a chunk of rock, he sat himself behind a prominent boulder leaning against another, with sufficient view of the battle scene to keep alert. In one sweeping scan, but not a casual sweep, he spotted one Indian, distant from all the others, on a black and white pony looping around to the left, riding low on the back of the pony the way many Indians did to keep a low profile ... and that path would bring the Indian in behind him … and in front of the patrol.

His mind jumped again. For brief seconds, full of white pictures, he was back in the mountains again in the middle of winter watching again yet another Indian; a lone Indian moving on the edge of vision, at once seen and then not seen; a moving, unseen enemy at times loaded with a threat to the life of others as well as his own.

The scene came back with full details: the sun burned on the edge of a mountain peak even as the cold snapped through his legs, went onto his hands trying to make fists, like a pair of unwanted gloves; onto his face as he felt the cold and saw the heat of the sun in one remarkable and dual sensation, thinking of opposites that ran alongside him in this life, ran without being deterred the least bit, ran with the speed of a runaway horse or a team of horses with the reins flapping loose in the air.

Thoughts ran toward duplication.

He tried to remember what he did that time; what made him do what he did; what pushed a decision to the top of his mind already clouded by disparate sensations from entirely different conditions.

The mountain Indian, obviously, had contraptions of some kind on his feet that allowed him to move on top of the deep snow. He had seen them before on mountain men, thinking they looked like flattened baskets. Something about that was working a similarity on him. He could feel it, even though the weather and the landscape and all the conditions were as different as they could be.

Now, as he looked again for the Indian, he saw him again as he dipped into a wadi, stayed out of site for a few minutes, re-appeared again, his form straight up in the saddle, only to duck again out of sight. The motions were repeated several times.

Luck came on him again as he thought about the sightings, the re-appearances, the sly acts not being so sly, or slyer than all of them together. The ruse of ruses, as old as the hills for sure.

By God, he said to himself, he wants me to see him. He wants to be seen. Immediately he thought again about the snow-runner in the mountains drawing his attention away from something else … and he thought about a mother bird faking a broken wing and drawing the fox away to wide grass, that near-broken wing flopping on the ground, looking helpless, flight an impossible outcome, fate sealed, all the while leaving her little hungry beakers in the nest further from danger with each minute.

There would be an attack from another quarter, he was positive.

Emberly made an appropriate signal to the guidon, noted the subtle response, the swift turn to report, the captain issuing an order by waving his hands, the ranks re-forming to face the left, arms at the ready, just in time to face an attack as a force of Indians rushed from a deep depression and rode in with wild screams and yells enough, usually, to unnerve any man.

The steady fire of the troops broke the rush, dropped some horses as well as riders, poured fire into the sudden messed up attack and drove it off. The scattered Indians rode off in several directions, but all away from the troops, and the lead scout out front now concentrating on the single Indian somewhere behind him.

Emberly's last sighting of him was behind a set of rocks such as he himself was hidden behind, so he concentrated on that location, eyeing the edges for slight giveaways. A slight movement caught his eye … the motion of a single feather completely vertical, and he knew it was worn by the Indian as a headdress piece.

With his own slyness, his horse tethered to a rock behind him, Emberly slipped into tall grass and came up unawares on the Indian's left side. There was no way he'd be able to hand-grasp the brave by himself, but he wanted a prisoner, so he fired one round into a rugged thigh. The brave fell to the ground, his rifle out of hand, but no scream issuing from him. As he rolled over on one side, his eyes staring at the soldier who caught him so easily, he nodded his acknowledgment even as he grimaced with the pain.

Standing over the fallen man, his rifle trained down on him, Emberly said, "You talk army talk?" He waited for a response and got none, so he continued, "You talk army talk with me who caught you like a rabbit in a snare and I will have army doctor fix your leg."

The wounded brave cast a grimace across his face, one first of anger, then of favor, and finally, with a twist of his lips, with agreement.

Emberly thought of a young squaw with a young son, sitting outside a lodge as she worked on the hide of a deer, her hands working it to a pliable touch, her eyes tender as she looked upon her child. The sorrow hit him as he realized there was no one waiting for him like that … the army never gave him the time, or the chance, to do so.

Pointing at the brave's rifle on the ground, Emberly said, "Where from?" He said it again, "Where from? From what man? Did you buy guns? Trade for guns?"

"Never buy. Get from soldier die on horse. Lose rifle."

"Where did you fight the soldiers?" Emberly said, looking out over the prairie, the distant mountains, placing his hand over his eyes as if to keep the sun out of them. "Where did you fight?"

The Indian's face showed a response before he spoke, the semi-smile touching with pride at his lips. "In Valley of the Lost Sun. Up there. In mountains." He said it as if he was pinning on a medal, a set of chevrons, placing a new feather in his headdress. He pointed to the far peaks.

In a twist of fate and chance, Emberly said, "Did you run on snow? Run fast on snow? Get behind troops? That was long ago. You look too young to be the runner on snow."

"I run on snow. You see me? You the one in the mountains?"

Emberly said, "We meet again. You have much courage to go alone. Two times you go alone."

"No. I go alone many times. I run faster than my brothers. Ride faster. Think faster. Brave is easy. Die is easy. Fight is hard. I get to see squaw and two papoose if I fight hard."

"Why do you fight so hard?"

"Soldier take our land. Our river. Our mountain. Soon our squaw. New papoose is not same papoose." His gaze was back over the long grass of the prairie. "When new papoose come new land come. New river come. New mountain come. New lodge come made of tree. Deer and buffalo hide go away."

He stopped talking and kept looking back at some distant sight, his eyes full of a new but old vision that Emberly imagined he too saw.

"What is your name?" Emberly said. "My name is Jacques Emberly."

"My name is Chase Puma."

Looking down at the brave, Emberly said, "Many brothers die here today."

"Die is easy. Fight is hard. Fight to see lodge in first sun. Fight to see squaw and papoose at lodge in first sun."

The rich thought of luck came on Emberly again. He knew he had another chance. He would not re-enlist, his mind suddenly made up. The firmness of that decision shook him. Down to his toes in his boots he felt it. And he saw the lodge in the first sun of another day. And the young squaw. And the two infants. And the wounded brave in front of him, wounded, that he had encountered for the second time that he knew. Maybe there might be a third time.

The long-time sergeant and scout, admirer of his foes and their bravery, put both rifles aside, dressed the wound as best he could, and said, "You stay here. Hide until soldiers go. Go see squaw and papoose when it is dark so you can see lodge in fist sun." He looked over his shoulder, saw nothing, heard nothing, and said, "Don't move until dark. Stay here. We might meet again."

Chase Puma said, "You see me two times now. I see you three times someday. Tirawa on high say man have second chance, third chance. Tirawa talk Pawnee from stars. Chase Puma hear Pawnee talk from stars."

Sergeant Jacques Emberly, lucky to his bones, rode off to get his discharge from the army in a matter of days. He never looked back at Chase Puma down in between rocks where he'd never be found by men on horseback, both men sharing the same vision of first sun and where it shone.

The Mogollons towered beside him for over three miles of trail when a cougar leaped from hiding. His horse reared, slipped and was tumbling. Noah Brittington fell off the edge of the trail, above Silver Creek, and went down into the mad current. He thought 16 years on this Earth was too short a lifetime for anybody to bear. If the good Lord was cheating him, what had he done for such a quick end, this simple run for gold? This trail was pointed out to him by his grandfather as the best way to the Mogollons and a cache of gold he had hidden away years earlier. But he had been lost for three days now. Was such a wise old man now lacking in wisdom or memory? Had he forgotten the right way? The weather was warm, the water would not freeze him, but would fill his boots that he'd have no way of getting off. The fall or sudden hit would wrench his weapons from their holsters, which might not be too bad for the swimming he hoped he could endure if he could stay clear of the horse hitting the water at the same time.

If ... if ... if ... water, not cold yet, but enveloping. Smothering.

Sixteen-year old Noah Brittington, his weapons quickly gone, went black as the horse pounded down into the stream directly beside him, brute legs thrashing at the threat, the sudden fall from surety. He never knew one hoof had collided with the back of his head. Did not know how much water he had swallowed. Did not know, for nearly an hour, that a young Indian brave had pulled him from the stream, had decided to save Noah rather than the horse the river was taking in its rapid flow.

The young grandson of an elderly prospector, now "out of the searchin' business," came to his senses on a warm, flat rock beside the bend where Silver Creek slowed its rush. The residue of sun's heat penetrated his backside first, then his bare arms. Shaking his head, his eyes starting to focus, he first saw the warm and inviting flames of a small fire, and then the face of the young Indian. The young brave, leaning over the fire, stirring it, a spit in front of him giving off a delicious aroma, was not the least afraid. That's when Noah B., as has mother called him, realized his pistols were gone, his rifle was gone, his horse was gone. He had only his clothes, a shirt drying on a thin stick of wood upright near the fire, his pants and boots drying in place on his body, his hat a cushion under his head.

The heat of the warm rock penetrated him before he sensed the heat of the fire. An awakening aroma of cooked meat filled the air. The Mogollon cliff was throwing down its first dark piece of shade; soon it would reach him and his companion.

The Indian, as young as he was, perhaps younger, held a piece of cooked meat out to him. Firelight sparkled in the brave's eyes. Noah B took the chunk of cooked meat gratefully, said, "Thank you," and began to gnaw in earnest. The Indian smiled and did the same, and in his almost full mouthful asked, "Who you?"

"Noah B."

"Nova Bee? That real name?" His teeth were brighter than any teeth Noah B had seen in a year or more. He vaguely remembered the smile on Sally Colamore's face, how her bright white teeth seemed so different from everybody else's teeth. At the back of his head, in a place almost dark, he saw her father's wagon, loaded high, passing by his grandfather's ranch as her family was on the way out of the territory, leaving forever.

Noah B looked around the thickening darkness. The water still flowed less than fifteen feet away, the sound steady though no longer in a rush. An unseen fish jumped and made a sound as it hit back at the blackening water. The shadows of the Mogollons as well as night itself reached out to touch the two young men, and fell across the fire. The overhead clouds gave off a promise of a break as a golden glow appeared in a rift. The moon was advancing through clouds and darkness.

"You pull me out?" Noah B made a swimming motion.

"I see you in water, looking down. No arms moving. Swim like Powatapha want me swim."

"Did I lose all my gear?" He touched his belt and empty holsters, shrugged his shoulders.

The Indian said, "River take all. Take horse down there." He pointed downstream. At the bend in the cliff Silver Creek was gone. So was his horse.

Noah B touched his own chest. "My name is No-ah B," he said. "Who are you?"

"I am son of Eagle Claw and Dew Morning. I am called River Walks. But only until I become chief. Then I will wear another name. I will pick the name from the mountain or the water. The mountain

44

and the river will sing my name. I will hear it when I am hunting for food, for skins, for the fish with many colors on his back. The wolf will run from me as he runs now, and the coyote, and the mad pig. The bird with arrow feathers in his wings will leave me signals against the sky."

Noah B, mystified by River Walks' natural reach at things, smiled at the litany, took another bite of meat, found interest as well as curiosity leaping within him. There was something old and pleasant and durable with the young Indian, obviously gathered from the ages and held close. Legend and myth had become an unbound book for him. His people, all the supposed diverse tribes and clans scattered from the snows of far Canada to the mountains below and beyond the big rivers, had been here a long time. All that was unwritten was still known. He wondered about all the things they might know that he'd never learn, not even hear about. Sally came back from wherever; maybe he'd never know about her. Maybe he'd never find the gold cache or see his mother or grandfather again.

"You remembering?" River Walks said. "Your eyes talk." His teeth were brighter yet, his smile real.

"I came here to help my grandfather, now a very old man with little to hold onto. He sent me to find what he had hidden here, a small treasure of the bright gold. He cannot work any longer. My father is dead, from endless work. I want to help my mother and my grandfather, so I came here to look for his cache."

"The old man is a chief, a dying chief?"

"In a way, yes, he is a chief. He is my chief. He is old as time." The vision of his grandfather locked on the small porch, his legs almost stiff now, his eyes narrowed when looking at him, trying to find his face, came in quick pictures at the back of his head. His grandfather's spirit would run all over the mountains if his legs would let him.

"He change his name when he become chief?"

Noah B thought he found an opening. "Yes," Noah B said, "now he is called Thunder Boss." The heavy and guttural voice of his grandfather came back to him like a shout from the mule end of a wagon. Now, at a distance, maybe not to be heard again, it was warm and comfortable. It gave his grandfather a solid sense of being in spite of the porch scene, the squinting eyes, the hands locked into ugly fists, the stiffening legs.

River Walks said, "He take his name from the sky? Is a big chief now, but send young man to get bright rock from the big mountain. I find bright rock in many caves of the big mountain, but no bright rock in the river. Mountain is big brother to river. River walks away from big brother. Take your horse, your guns, fill your mouth with water only Powatapha know how much, send me."

"You know the bright rock?" Noah B said with deep interest. Perhaps his luck had not run out on him with the fall. Firelight flickered across River Walks face, young on the skin, old in the eyes.

"Cougar stand guard on bright rock. He watches for the mountain. Knew you were coming on the trail. I know all the way from other side. Saw cougar watching you. If you take heart of the mountain, cougar try to take it back."

"We use the bright rock. We get food with bright rock. You do not value bright rock?"

"It belongs to mountain. We do not take it from mountain."

"You take mountain's deer for food. Mountain bird eggs from nests. They live and die, sometimes you kill them. I just take bright rock that has no life in it to give life."

River Walks smiled at Noah B. "You talk like old Indian getting older. I know the talk you say. I have heard it at council fire since I was young. My father wants to live in the mountains and get older as the sun gets colder. He does not want more wars. Powatapha makes all men brothers but not all brothers know they are brothers. All Indians come across the bridge of ice the way Powatapha lead them. He lead them past the ice to the happy mountains where ice does not stay all the time. Powatapha let them see how things grow, how sky throw down sun and rain, light and dark, warm and cold. Some brothers of the nations fight among themselves. They forget Powatapha brought them all from the land of the ice over the ice bridge."

"Did Powatapha know bright rock was here? Did he leave it for me to use, but not for you? Does the cougar keep you away as he keeps me away?"

"You talk council talk. My father would know your words, but not all at council would believe. I know your talk. I will take you to bright rock in the new sun. You take it to old chief, Big Thunder Boss, tell him no war here."

"I will do that, River Walks. Noah B promises that." He saw

46

the rift in the clouds, the moon poking through, a gold and silver moon touching the raggy edges of clouds, the raggy edges of the Mogollon cliff, touching the strange companionship of Indian and cowboy, both youths with a hopeful outlook.

"I lose my knife in river," River Walks said, "or we could become blood brothers." Instead of using a knife, he unwound a cord that was about his neck. "Put around your wrists, and you will never break our bond. You try and break."

He wrapped the cord about Noah B's wrists, holding them tightly together. Though the cord was thin, Noah B could not break it. He struggled, twisting it all the time, even putting his arms over his head. He could not break the thin cord. He tried the overhead maneuver again, without luck.

That's when the shot rang out, from across the river. River Walks fell down on the flat rock. A voice rang out. "We got him, Noah. We got him. Hurry, boys, in case he ain't dead yet. Hang on, Noah, we're comin'."

"No," Noah screamed. "He's my friend. He's my friend."

Silence came across Silver Creek. Overhead, the raggy clouds closed on the moon.

Noah B fell across the body of River Walks. He was crying when the men got to him, his hands still trussed in the thin cord.

Dead Pony Lookout

Darkly Armitage, astride Bullet, a magnificent stallion he had corralled himself when he was just 16 years old, sat atop Dead Pony Lookout, a two day ride from the Bar-B ranch where he earned his pay and keep these days, just a scad over his 20th birthday. Rustlers had been active for more than three months in many points of the territory and cautions were about. The marshal said he thought all the troubles were being done at the hands of different pieces of the same gang. Their timing was more than adequate to fluster posses and private searches, "coming," like he said, "at opposite ends of the clock and the compass... morning here, night there; northerly here, southerly there." Darkly had been posted by Bar-B boss Devon Armstrong and his wife Barbara to a week long search for any signs of the gang.

"Why's the place called Dead Pony Lookout?" Darkly Armitage said. "I've seen the place from the top of Crater Peak and that's got a better and a longer view, but I never heard why the name and no interest until now." He shrugged his shoulders the way cowboys use physical punctuation at times.

"Sure," Armstrong replied, "and it'll take you a whole damn day just to get down from the peak to flat side. So, get yourself up to Dead Pony Lookout when you're ready, but here's what I know." He then told Darkly, in some detail, what he had heard from others about Dead Pony Lookout. It was an extensive story.

To Darkly's inquisitive mind, Dead Pony Lookout appeared to be nothing but a story that had come off the big grass and a late campfire, or a late jug of good tastin'. When he got to the Lookout he found no way to get Bullet up to the top, no way at all. Darkly tied him off below, gave him some water and spent half an hour in the climb, on a series of steps and small recesses carved into the stonework. At the top was a small flat butte area no bigger than a barnyard, with a long view across grass and a river and a ravine siding the bigger climbs into the mountain range in the distance.

Talking to himself, he said, "There's no way anybody found a pony up here, dead or alive. Some injun types long ago made the climb up here by cutting or chipping their way up, with those stairs or what's left of them now. But there's no way they got a pony up here, or anybody after them. It ain't proper belief." All that talk echoed in the back of his mind, the way some things never let go, like a girl's name way off in another territory or a past lifetime, or a horse's name, or a pard that did a big favor one time when trouble came around like a tumble weed on the prowl, or strays after wild lightning cut loose on a whole chunk of territory.

He tried to remember everything that Armstrong had told him about The Lookout. "A couple of troopers from the cavalry heard about the place from an old Indian guide. 'Bad medicine for any people go up there,' the guide'd said. 'Pawnee people make medicine to pony that die up there, hit by lightning after getting to top with chief. Both chief and pony die, but the tribe bring the chief down to put him in special burial ground. For a long time they make medicine at the top around the dead pony.' Anyway, the troopers who went up there and found the dead pony skeleton were killed a few days later by injuns, like the bad medicine promised for anyone who climbed to the top, the holy ground for injun animals. Bones of the pony were found where he fell down dead in the beginning or was killed by some evil means, any guess would do. But the word about the place kind of spread itself around a long time ago before you came into the territory. At first it went from fireplace to fireplace, saddle to saddle, ranch house to ranch house and then died out. Others had died after climbing up there, they say, but that's all from a long time ago. A long time ago." Armstrong tossed off the last part as if everything up to then was just a joke.

Darkly understood it all as a challenge to him, because Armstrong then said, "Of course, if you believe all that kind of crap, it'll get under your craw. Otherwise, it's just another long view of things that litter the mind."

In the recesses of Darkly's mind, he promised himself to think real heavy about all the stuff he had heard, whether any of it was true or was a made-up thing. He told himself to be aware of all options that could find a place to work.

Quickly back on the job, Darkly ran over the necessities of the day; he had to keep Bullet watered, keep his eye out for rustlers or strange bands of riders, figure out how many times he would have to make the climb up and down and keep it at a minimum, keep moving while on top because the buzzards from a hundred miles away could spot a still body. At length realized he'd have to spend the night below and not on top of Dead Pony Lookout. A coffee fire up on top was an alarm signal to those he was looking for. It would also demand a load

49

of firewood be carried up, which he could do without, in a whole hurry.

With nothing visible on top of the butte, no remnants of any visitors, including the dead pony, he began to look around the site. It was one way to keep moving because he had seen one buzzard in the far sky, and one buzzard meant dozens of them in a matter of minutes.

Then, in one small recess at the edge, as if tucked there by someone or had fallen into that place, or actually dropped by one of the vultures, he found a bone, a large bone. It was not human, he was sure, and then thought it was actually from a small horse... or a pony. A pony's leg bone. It creased his mind with heavy thinking, even as he watched the far skylines, the sky, the spread of the earth below as it swept off to the far mountains. He'd descend soon, he decided, as evening offered its small announcements; a bird's song not far away, a cloud appearing thicker than it really was, a shadow astride an edge of the land at a distance.

Darkly pictured himself tossing the bone over the side of the butte, but thought better of it: if the bone was part of a ceremonial act, it had a right to be in its own place. He felt adamant about that, believing the one God above set the store for all those who roamed the earth seeking their final elsewhere.

At that moment, as if all things were so ordained for him on this day, including some strange answers, he saw a small cloud of dust rising on the far horizon. He went prone on the top of Dead Pony Lookout, his eye steady on the dust as it swirled higher, thicker, less than an hour's ride from where he was. At a point where evening began and day ended, at the mark of a mountain turning in on itself, he could make out the dust, and attached cattle or horses, disappearing into a point between two very similar peaks. He could mark them from anywhere he might choose.

His report to Armstrong back at the Bar-B ranch was hardly finished when a whole posse of lawmen, volunteers, cattle men in particular, mounted en masse and rode out, Darkly Armitage out front like a bird dog or an injun scout.

It ended up in a shoot-out of some great proportions, in a blind canyon in the mountains, about an hour's ride from Dead Pony Lookout. A lot of lead was thrown around the hidden canyon. A few gents on both sides got injured, and one magnificent black stallion, not Bullet, was killed by a rampaging steer. Over 1000 head of cattle were recovered from the canyon, as were a hundred or so horses from various remudas, with every local brand visible. There followed the incarceration of a dozen rustlers who threw down their weapons as the heavy numbers of cattle owners and ranch hands moved in on them.

When all the fighting was finished, the cattle settled back with their owners, as well as the hundred or so horses, the rustlers awaiting their fate in jail cells, Armstrong said to Darkly Armitage, once they were back at the Bar-B ranch, "What do you think about the story of Dead Pony Lookout now, Darkly? Can you believe some of that injun stuff? Remember, they were here long before we got here." He had struck a pose between the real and the mythic, about as far as some arguments can get about Indians, and about as close.

"The whole thing was a set-up, boss," Darkly said. "I figure them injuns, smarter than some of us by a whole wagonload, found a dead pony, let the meat go as carrion to the vultures or whatever eats dead meat, and then they carried the bones up to the top of the butte and dropped them in some kind of skeleton remainder or form, like the pony hisself had died on the spot from a bolt of lightning, along with the famous chief of some name. The truth gets staggered from then on, but we make of it what they want us to."

Darkly Armitage had covered a lot of ground and decided to finish. "All kinds of stuff like that come into play. There's no ghosts out there, and no magicians, and no tribe's witch doctors, only thankful people who make sense at times, or make it seem so, for their everlasting benefit."

Armstrong nodded as if he had an understanding of the whole charade.

"It's as simple as all that," Darkly Armitage said, ending in his mind any argument about Dead Pony Lookout.

Everyone in his hometown in Colorado said he was a winner, he'd get it all, and here he was flat on his back hiding in deep brush; gone were his horse, his holstered guns and rifle, his hat and canteen. The only thing he had held onto was the rope his hand fell on when his horse was shot out from under him. The horse fell down a ravine and he hoped the big gray was dead before hitting the ground; he'd been a good mount for five years.

Chad Lumsden could hear someone scavenging down below; there'd go his saddle, reins, weapons, and canteen - his survival possessions.

He caught the whinny of a horse somewhere below on the trail, but not in the ravine. Then he heard a horse pass by above him and realized at least two ambushers had had their eyes on him. He held his breath, hardly daring to breathe. That single ball of held breath was like a firepot at the moment, and Lumsden had to let some of it go, hoping the horseman above had moved on. Out his nostrils, as quietly as possible, he let that air go, and felt his nerves tighten, muscles tense up, found a prayer come pursed on his lips.

His mind shot eastward toward the small ranch in the sequestered valley of Chasm Country. It was pretty country with good pasture running into the foothills. It was memorable country.

And it was learning country.

"Listen, Sonny," his father had said, one day not far from the ranch house, "it won't always be as good as it is now. Times will change and so will the chances. It's the way the cards are dealt to us. You got to be ready for the changes. That's the biggest and most important thing in life ... you got to be ready for the changes. Sometimes they'll come at you like rocks in an avalanche, so you'll know them when you see them or hear them, 'cause you'll probably have to duck. Others most likely are going to sneak up on you like dawn does some days."

His father's hand had, from horseback, reached out and tapped him gently on the arm. It carried the tone, for his father, not a touching man but a good man and responsible, had stressed his words with that touch. In this new moment of recall he'd swear he could feel that hand practically anoint him again, with the words echoing as they had ever since being said.

With a slight hesitation, he tried to remember why he was up here, in the hills, in the first place. Rhyme and reason kept their distance, and he stayed in the quandary, nothing coming clear to him. The knot on his head helped him to decide that he had forgotten something; he couldn't bring it back.

He had a length of rope off his pommel – and that was it. Him and the rope.

Something was trying to break through, but he couldn't open the door for it. Then he laughed softly as he realized he also had his good luck piece, the tinny toy flute his grandfather had given him years ago, saying, "Play a few notes on this when your good luck is at hand" – pause – "or if it's left you high and dry or down and out."

Lumsden, at that moment, also heard the clatter of a horse's hoofs. The mount was on the stone part of the trail, above him, heading for the open rim where Saltersville could be seen in the distance. He had seen the town before from that same site.

For a few moments Lumsden reflected on a lot of memories, some good and some bad, and listened as silence slipped into the mountains and a slight shift of air said that evening was coming on, and possibly a cool night. He had to get under cover as soon as he could.

Just below the ridge line at the edge of the brush where he was hiding, he saw an opening, either a cave or at least an overhanging ledge. Gambling on finding a decent place at least for the coming night, he scrounged a bundle of fire wood and roped it down, pulled the rope back up and let himself down, with the rope looped off in place. If he had to, he could climb back up with the help of the rope, which he tied off on a piece of fallen rock.

He found a small cave in the canyon wall. It was empty of critters, and when night set in, he lit a small fire, and fell asleep. Dawn woke him, rested but a bit chilly, the fire long died out.

Lumsden studied his situation again; there was only one way out, but was it up or down?

In the clear morning breakthrough, the sun splashing on peaks above him, a new sound came to him. All the intelligence he owned told him it was Indians on the move. They'd surely find the rope looped around a part of the ledge above. He slowly pulled on one end and the length of rope slid down to his hands – meaning any escape for him was now downward.

Lumsden backed deeper into the cave when he realized the Indians must have seen the movement of the rope, or smelled him or the cold ashes of his fire. He backed into the cave as far as he could go, the aperture beyond too slim to pass through, footsteps sounding in the otherwise silent morning.

He heard again his grandfather saying, as much prophecy as could be, "Play a few notes on this when your good luck is at hand" – pause – "or if it's left you high and dry or down and out."

Toy flute came into his hand as if it had been delivered to him by the Pony Express.

He raised it to his lips and started a tinny sound, finding some moments of magic as the homely music sailed through the small aperture behind him, rose atop a stony but resonant surface and stopped the Indians' approach in place, as the eerie music issued from another aperture. The mountain came alive with magic, as accompaniment to the voice of the god Wantatowee or Manitowak or whoever held sway on this mountain.

The good luck won out for Lumsden. Looking down he saw some of the natives drop the gear they had stripped from his dead horse. One of them brought up a horse, a paint pony, and saddled him, hung all his gear appropriately, and tied the horse off on a rock. Then the five of them climbed out of sight, leaving salvation behind in the ravine – as if the god of the mountain had condemned them, ordered them, thanked them with music from the heart of the mountain.

He did not see any of the Indians again; they had slipped away into some part of the mountain as if they had been commanded to disappear.

The paint was gentle, strong, and accepted him as Lumsden mounted and rode out of the ravine. In a few hours he was entering the saloon in Saltersville.

The barkeep and owner, Harry Fontaine, greeted him. "Well, well, Chad, we thought we might have lost you for a while there. Folks said you were gone near two days. You got some special story you're willin' to tell us? We're all ears for that one, son, but glad to have you back at the same time." He poured a mug of beer and set it on the counter. "Your pa was mighty nervous, like he had ants in his pants. Left here twice and came back and had another beer with us both times. Nerves lookin' for company I guess. Y'oughtn't to do that to your pa. He lost some shine them two days."

"You wouldn't believe me, Harry, what I'd have to tell and the Indians up there in the mountains. They're not any plain Plains Indians. There's something special about them."

Fontaine jumped right in and said, "You ain't been talkin' to them alone, have you, Chad? Ain't much safety in that. They'd leave you so even your pa wouldn't know you."

"You're wrong there, Harry. You're looking at me now and they could have had me easy as you please."

He proceeded to tell Fontaine about the events on the mountain, right down to the tune he was playing on the toy flute.

Fontaine, going right past the story about the music, said, "No idea about who was shootin' at you, Chad?"

"Not a flicker of who. I saw nothing. Just heard them looking for me when I was hiding in the brush. Probably at least two bushwhackers waiting to clean out my pockets." He flipped the talk. "What do you think about the Indians and how they just quit trying to get me and even saddled up a horse for me?"

"Maybe thought you was a god come alive for them, like Mawawawa, or Wamamama." Fontaine added a healthy snicker to his fun-and-games name-poking at the Indian gods.

"That's pretty funny from where you sit, Harry, but don't ask me to laugh. They let me be and for a reason I may never know, but am thankful."

"They're just plain old Indians, Chad. Nothin' to get excited about."

"Except I'm still alive. And I'll tell you this, Harry, that I'm going back up there someday."

Chad told his father the whole story and what he wanted to do, and on his own.

The kindly older gent agreed to all, happy that his lone son had been spared up in the mountains, by the god of the mountains.

Three months later the local freighter brought a package to the Lumsden ranch, all the way from Independence, Missouri. It was addressed to "Chad Lumsden, Lumsden Ranch, near Saltersville, Colorado."

The next day, Chad Lumsden packed an extra horse with the package, a few blankets, and other supplies, including five extra ropes, and rode off to the mountains where he had almost lost his life. His errand was peaceful and thankful.

With guile, strength and determination, he managed to get his supplies and the package up to the same place where he had spent a lonely night, and a miraculous escape.

He managed to haul up some fire wood, lit a fire at darkness, and went to sleep beside the fire.

As before, he awoke, rested but chilly, and a little nervous. But he was adamant about completing his errand.

He backed into the fissure, as he had before, when he heard movement on the trail.

The flute came to his mouth, and his three months of practice on the tin flute produced a remarkable piece of music. The sounds of that music resonated on rock faces up through the connecting fissures in and through the mountain. The music resounded with miraculous acoustics that few Indians had ever dreamed of.

When they came along the ravine below him and along the ledge above him, Chad Lumsden brought out the package from Missouri, opened it, and took out 100 tin flutes. For more than an hour he sat on the ledge playing flute after flute, which the Indians admired as if the god of the mountain was playing it himself.

After the hour of playing, one Indian advanced toward him down below and held up his hand in the sign of peace. Lumsden tied a rope on the package of flutes and lowered it to the floor of the ravine. The Indian, the same one who had placed Lumsden's saddle on the paint pony months earlier, picked up the package, mounted his horse and rode away.

In a matter of minutes, not a single Indian was visible. Chad Lumsden rode his own horse back to Saltersville, met his father at the saloon where each of them had a beer, and 50 years later was still telling the story about the musical mountain every chance he could.

Part Sioux, Part Soldier

Arizona Tyle, rancher along the Squash River, rode into Fort Sunbury screaming that his wife Olive had been taken by Indians while he was chasing down loose horses up along the river. His two ranch hands had been driving a small herd of cows down the river to meet up with other stock.

"She was only alone for a few hours," he said to the captain, "Everything's been quiet for months. No sign of any Indians. I tried to trail them, but when they crossed the river, I lost them. I could be looking for them all day, so I thought I better come in here and get some help."

Captain Harry Mason saw how distraught Tyle was, and feared for the safety of his wife. He was also worried that the quiet sector he oversaw would be disrupted by a single event. He had no doubt that a major problem could break out at any time, and for any reason. With that state of mind, he decided that a force rushing from the fort would be seen as too heavy an action, and would result in political problems. It all sounded to the captain that the immediate emergency should be placed at first into the hands of one man of trust.

Captain Mason said to his chief scout, Private Bent Red Fox, "You know his place, Private. Go take a look and see what you can find. We'll catch up to you later on." He could have choked on his words, knowing they carried little truth in them.

Bent Red Fox, in a quick survey of Tyle's property not far from the river, found the trail leading away from the ranch to where the raiding party entered the river. He did not waste any time searching for where they came out of the water, but headed immediately for the range of mountains and rolling hills running off to the north. Indian ways were known to him, all Indian ways, including how they thought and planned moves and campaigns, how they would elude pursuing enemies, what false signs they would leave in their wake. Indians had the ability to divert superior forces time after time, for they knew the land, scouted the enemy at all times, and believed in the messages sent to them by great gods of the earth and sky.

In a matter of several hours, working on his special knowledge of Indian traits and tendencies, Private Bent Red Fox, chief scout for Captain Harry Mason's 5th Brigade of the western frontier, alone on a crest of Tattle Mountain, looked down on an Indian encampment in a sheltered valley and saw the blonde Tyle woman tied to a young sapling at the edge of a copse of trees. He could not believe the Indians were Crows, not this far south out of Montana, even though most of the dress and regalia they wore said they were Crows from Montana. Studying some of the braves, he admitted they looked like Crows, walked like Crows, with that certain pride and disdain they could mount. Some of the braves wore leather leggings and buckskin shirts and some of the women wore deerskin dresses. He saw the fringes on the dresses, and guessed they looked like quills and large elk teeth Crows used to adorn their clothing.

But some of these Indians, these supposed Crows, were not dressed the same way. The differences were too far apart to satisfy a keen eye, and Bent Red Fox had a keen eye. Something was wrong with the scene. Crows, as far back as he knew, were not braggarts though they were proud, and did not enjoy the punishment of any woman who could possibly bring a child to the band, to add to the Nation. But the blonde Tyle woman bound to a tree would get cold and sick before the night ahead of them came to an end.

Making sure there would be no reflection from the looking glass he was about to use, Bent Red Fox focused the glass on the woman. The view proved that she was the wife of the rancher who had ridden into the compound screaming that the Indians, Crows he was sure, had captured his wife and all his horses. Bent Red Fox had seen the woman before, in the fort getting supplies. If he left to get help now, they would be long gone, disappearing into the hills of Nations, before he could get back with help. And the woman might never be found.

It was all up to him, to try to arrange or plan some kind of release for the woman, to help her escape her certain fate. It would be up to his Sioux skills, not his soldier skills; that argument found no contradiction in his mind.

He watered his horse and sat to eat a light meal while his mind kept going over the scene. The view with the glass showed that none of the braves wore paint always worn for rites, raids or war, and in special fashions. Then he noticed that none of shirts on the braves looked very colorful or unique, often true of Crow shirts, finely done and so dazzling in their making. None of the shirts in the encampment looked like they had been made by the Apsaalooke Crows. In fact, he remembered Mandan and Flathead shirts were just like the shirts the braves in the encampment were wearing.

What was afoot, he wondered.

At one end of the encampment he spotted five braves fixing weapons and his eye told him he was looking at a Sioux work party. Many such work parties had he seen as a boy and taken part in as he matured. Clothing on the working braves was Sioux clothing without a doubt.

Out of one tipi came the only brave in the whole encampment who was wearing a war bonnet, a tall, feathered headdress that hung well down his back. "That," Bent Red Fox said, "is the chief of this band of Indians."

Then he realized he was looking at a composite war party of the famous Crow chieftain, Flying Bear, the escaped killer of a soldier general a full year earlier in a Plains encounter. In succeeding raids after his escape from an Army fort prison, Flying Bear had freed over 100 captured Indians and brought them under his command. They waged war on all whites they came in contact with and the growing band had been on the loose for almost six full moons, raising havoc in many hit and run raids looking for horses, ammunition and other supplies.

Flying Bear, he was convinced, would not let the captured woman bring a child to the Nation. He would let her suffer like so many Indian maidens and squaws had suffered at the hands of white men. But it was not right that a woman should not have a child in her life, and this rancher Tyle's wife, he figured, had no children. Bent Red Fox believed with a deep conviction that all women should have a chance at bearing children.

His also knew that neither bravery nor stupidity would get freedom for the woman. The Indians down below were courageous to a man, and would not be afraid of any brave or stupid act he alone could bring against them. He would have to go to the heart of their beliefs to gain her freedom. He had to trick them.

As he finished his light meal of jerky, he counted his options and his supplies. Sixty rounds of ammunition for rifle and sidearm were in his pack, along with a flask of gunpowder, and two sticks of dynamite he had found at an abandoned mining site during this search, with fuses for exploding them. The ammunition would inflict little damage on the Indians before he'd be killed. So they were discounted. Only the dynamite looked to be a possibility, but would have to be accompanied by a dent in Indian beliefs and customs.

He would have to find a way to penetrate their thinking, to divert their obvious aims.

Looking down at the encampment again, the Sioux in him told him he was looking at the preparations for a ritual of some sort. Flying Bear was seated on a stump with two maidens on each side. Fire had been brought to place in front of him and the fire was fed by one of the maidens with light sticks or twigs every few minutes to keep bright the orange-red flames.

The ritual was underway.

With a dramatic motion, Flying Bear had the woman brought before him and staked to the ground. Then began a ritual of asking for a sign from on high about how the woman should be disposed of. Flying Bear stood over her, his right arm pointing down at her, his left arm raised to the heavens, imploring that a sign be sent to him. With his arms flapping like a wounded bird, Flying Bear circled around the woman seven times, asking for seven words to direct him. Bent Red Fox knew the ceremony, had learned it from his mother who had escaped such a predicament in her younger life.

He wanted that woman to have a child of her own, as his mother had.

Flying Bear, he believed, would wait for a sign.

Bent Red Fox gathered enough dry brush to form an arrow pointing down to earth and arranged it all on the side of the hill. At the point of the arrow he placed the dynamite so that its fuse would be exposed to the flames when the brush was ignited. Then he ignited the collection of dry twigs and brush.

The pile ignited slowly, at both ends and began to burn down to the point. There was a lot of activity in the encampment and Flying Bear, pointing up at the arrowed flames, grabbed a bow and an arrow from a brave and pointed down at the woman. All his actions said he was going to kill her with an arrow.

He had drawn the arrow back upon its leather cord and was apparently about to shoot the arrow into the woman, as the gods had directed him from high above, when the dynamite went off. The explosion rocked the mountain, sounding as if a terrible voice was upset with the entire world beneath it.

Flying Bear and all his cohorts broke camp in a hurry and left the area, with the woman still staked to the ground, left to die in any way the gods would choose, rather than the way an Indian had interpreted a sign.

The whole encampment of Indians was gone about two hours when Bent Red Fox, halfway down the hill, noticed a peccary nosing about the area. He shot it with a single round from his rifle. For at least an hour he watched to see if there was anybody lingering from the departed encampment. When there was no other movement or sign of any Indian from Flying Bear's followers he, in short order, freed the woman from the stakes and set off for the fort with her on the saddle behind him. Her arms were wrapped around his waist and lightly tied in place so she would not fall off the saddle. She was very weak, made no talk, but managed a sigh now and then.

When the pair rode into the fort, a great welcome and acclaim arose for them, from the other Indian scouts, from all the troops, from the commanding officer who saluted the returning scout, and from the husband of the rescued woman who helped her down from the saddle when her hands were loosened. The grateful husband thanked Bent Red Fox and then hugged his wife again.

Bent Red Fox said, "Do you and your wife have children?" He wanted to assure his stance in the matter.

"No," the husband said, "but I don't think we'll have to wait too long, though, with many thanks to you."

"I am glad for you and your wife," Bent Red Fox said as he shook hands with the man again and nodded at the man's wife. "It is good for woman to have children. They carry life to a new place."

A lone rider, Parker Cartbridge, on his way home from visiting a comrade wounded during the Civil War that ended three years earlier, came up out of a wadi and saw the column of smoke far down the river. The smoke rose almost arrow-straight, not an extra breath of air to be known coming down from the mountain or across the river. He closed down on the source, riding in an easy manner, alert, his horse Big Jip enjoying the leisurely moves. Rugged as stone in his features, Cartbridge was broad at the brows that were thick as maize, alert of eyes and ears with slight movements of his head, and sat the saddle as if he was born in it. His alertness on the trail was a sign of the times; readiness was the first requirement, and demand, of any man on the move. Brigands and road agents and renegades had been around for a long time, but in this part of Wyoming they had thinned out in recent years, as well as Indian surprises.

But fate works in lonely ways at times, and in lonely hours.

"Easy, Jip, slow and easy. You tell me if anything's around, anything alive." The man was looking at the burning remains of a small Indian village, most of the teepees down and gone to ash, embers still smoldering, nothing else moving. Cartbridge worked for extra air, drawing some of it deeply into his lungs, knowing the taste of death in it. The smell of a Vicksburg field came back to him swift as a shot, for beyond the smell of death there came comrade Leroy Palmer stretching his hand to him one last time, death making itself known to both of them.

Cartbridge wondered what kind of memories lingered out in front of him now, in the remnants of the village, trying to imagine what had set off the scene, which came to him as pure annihilation. Such things he had seen before.

He shook off comrade Palmer's last image just as Big Jip stopped in his tracks, his ears standing at attention on the magnificent black head. The horse pawed the ground as if he was using sign language.

The man heard nothing, saw nothing, but understood the basic message. "You sure, Jip?" he said. His voice was low and without alarm. Patting the horse, Cartbridge sent his own message of trust in return.

The horse stood his ground, his ears working, but his tail

hanging still. One leg was held in the raised position, the way a comma works in a sentence, or a breath is held. Jip slowly placed that hoof on the ground.

At that moment Cartbridge heard, faint as the traces of a forgotten breeze from a day earlier, an infant's whimpers. The cries seemed to come from a blow-down that had fallen across the remains of another blow-down. The tangled mass, like night at its core, conveyed secrets in the thick shadows.

The cries came again, a little stronger, yet plaintive, like loon he heard once across a lake, as though the cries were calling for help.

Dismounting, dropping a rein on a bare limb and retrieving his rifle from its saddle sling, Cartbridge poked the rifle bore-first into the clutter of dead leaves and branches. A surprise came into his vision; an Indian infant was lying on its mother's chest. The mother's eyes were wide open, stuck with fright and locked into death. He closed her lids and withdrew the infant who was wearing a single buckskin garment adorned with some type of drawing burned on it, perhaps an animal. The baby was only months old, he could tell, with black hair already thick with promise. The gray eyes looked up at him. The infant whimpered again, and then fell asleep in the crook of the man's left arm. His right hand was free beside his holster, as it always was out on the trail.

On the trail back to his ranch, Jip moving comfortably under him, the man looked down at the baby who continued to sleep. He admired the dark hair, the bright complexion as if the sun had shone on the face for long hours, and the curve at the child's lips. A personality, he assured himself, was being developed.

"Oh," he said as Big Jip lengthened stride, smelling water at the ranch's dammed creek, "Cybil will love this one." He was not sure if he should say her or him, not daring to check now that he was on the move, afraid he would drop the precious cargo. He drew the little one closer. "Oh, my," he said, "this will be Cybil's birthday present."

It all flashed back at him, the way Leroy Palmer had entered his mind, coming home to Cybil after the war was over, his release from the hospital, and her rushing out of the ranch house as he rode up along the fence line in his dark blue uniform. "My childless wife," he had muttered. "How do I tell her what's happened to me?"

That puzzle was lost in their excitement that day as she almost pulled him from his horse.

Only later had he told her that he would not be able to give her the child she wanted so much. "We'll do with what we have," she assured him that night. "We'll find a way to get along. We always have. This war has been a hell for us, but we are here, and it is now."

She smiled the smile he had carried in the back of his head for three long years, through a dozen battles, only sharing some of its being with Leroy Palmer on the last day of his life. The spark of her being was still evident and he knew why he had fallen in love with her when they were young as pups, and why Palmer had also smiled a one-time smile saying he understood his comrade's luck.

Now, again, Cartbridge rode along the fence line, carrying the infant who had just awakened as if the smell of an apple pie had been shared. The aroma wove itself through the air, the baby cried, and Cybil was standing on the porch, her hands on her hips, the white apron halving her green outfit. The evening sun played about her. The grass was rich and green. He was home again.

"Parker Cartbridge," Cybil said, her hands out in front of her as she heard the cries again, "what do you have in your arms?" Cartbridge knew she was half afraid of the answer, and half expectant of a major surprise. Cybil Cartbridge always had a special way about her.

"It's an Indian baby I found out there at the great bend of the river where the mountains meet. It looks like a small village of Indians was surprised by a raiding party and this little one is all that's left, far as I know."

He handed the infant to its new mother, who took a look under the buckskin garment. "It's a boy," she said, and hugged him to her breast. Her face was as glorious as a morning sunrise, her eyes as compassionate as Cartbridge had ever seen them. Warmth kindled itself within him.

In a quick decision, that came out as a question, she said, "What do we call him?"

"You have the honor, Cybil. You give him a name. From this moment, he belongs to you. You tell me how you want it handled, what I tell people. You make the decision."

"The honest truth, that's all. He's an orphan that came to us. That's it." And as part of her quick decision, she added, "and his name will be Roy, in honor of your comrade Leroy Palmer."

"Roy Cartbridge?" he said.

64

"From now on, little sweetheart," she said to the bundled infant, "you are Roy Cartbridge."

She turned on her heels and rushed off into the next part of her life.

Roy Cartbridge was taught much in his early years, learned about all of it, and grew into a fine young man coming up on his fifteenth year. He was as dark-haired as his father, said people who did not know of the boy's start in life, and carried himself with the same kind of confidence that Parker Cartbridge was noted for. Often they worked in tandem at a single chore, as good as any two ranch hands in the whole of Wyoming.

Roy said one day when the pair was working on a new corral section, "Pa, you notice that old Indian that comes around once in a while? I've seen him twice or three times in the last year or so, but yesterday, when I was skinning some of these poles, I saw him closer than any time before. I don't see many Indians around here since the army moved up to new place on the river."

Parker Cartbridge, aware for a lot longer than young Roy about the old Indian, said, "I've seen the old buck for a lot of years. Many times on an old sorrel, and then on foot a number of times. I figure he lives somewhere in the mountains and stretches his legs once in a while. Too old to cause any trouble, I'd bet. He's probably a hundred years old and knows everything he ever learned."

"I bet he'd be interesting to talk to," Roy said. "I can just imagine what he's learned over the years. Lot more than I have. Heck, I just learned how to skin a deer last year. He must have done that when he was a lot younger than me."

Cartbridge digested the logic in Roy's words, and then said, as if in self-defense, "He doesn't know how to brand a cow, I'd think."

"What for, Pa? Why'd they want to brand a cow? They don't keep a herd, but probably eat what they want only when they need it."

"I'd say you were right on that point, Roy. Why don't we ask him in the next time we see him. That would be a good idea. Your mother would have the same feelings, I'm sure."

So it was, a few weeks later, that the only two survivors of the massacred Indian village, at the great bend of the river, came together on a foothill of the mountain range near the Cartbridge ranch. And fifteen years after the sad event.

65

"My name is Roy Cartbridge," he said to the old Indian he came upon walking away from a small stream with a catch of trout over his shoulder, a rawhide line running through their mouths and out their gill slots. "My father and I have seen you a number of times out here. He said I should ask you to come to visit us at the ranch, either now or whenever you feel like it. Eat with us at the ranch. You have history all around you."

He liked the stately looks of the old Indian. Must have been a chief, he thought, as the old man held up his hand in a sign of friendship.

"I am Kiowa," the Indian said. "My name is Eagle One-claw. I live alone up there all warm weather and cold weather, in a cave." He pointed uphill. "I have many skins to keep me warm, many hides. I eat eggs, rabbit, goat, a lost cow in the ravines when it snows heavy. Sometimes a bear." There was a smile on his face, as if expecting the boy's next question.

"How do you catch a bear?" Roy Cartbridge's eyes were wide open with contemplated wonder. His dark brows accented his wonder, gave his face a new look, a new esteem.

The old Indian let a smile make its way on his face, followed by a nod that carried many unsaid words. "I let bear chase me, then drop rocks on him I gather all summer. Big piles of rocks in many place. Try not to get caught alone by bear or puma. They chase me, I hurt them, make them bait or eat them."

Roy Cartbridge shook his head in awe. "You are a very smart and brave man, and so wise to be able to live alone with no relatives around you, no one from the tribe. My father will be pleased to meet you. My mother, too. She is a great cook. She bakes pies I can smell all the way out on the wide grass."

"All Indians are smart. You right when you say Indians, like Kiowa, have history with them all the time. We bring it to all the tribe to know. Indian born with it." The warm smile came again, and the accenting nod of his head. "I know smell of apples out on the grass. It is a warm smell that say apple. I have known it many times."

The fuzziest feeling Roy Cartbridge ever knew came rising in him, as if he was being immersed in a new river, a new body of water, in a ceremony. His skin tingled. His fingers trembled to touch something he had no knowledge about but could feel. There came the fleeting thought that asked how close the old Indian had come to the ranch house, as though more than apple pie aroma and curiosity might have pulled him. He didn't know the comfort of the gods had called on him.

At the ranch house, Eagle One-claw ate sparingly, taking his time, letting conversation control the time of the meal. He kept staring at Roy Cartbridge during the meal, which made Cybil say, on the spur of the moment, "Roy, our son, was given to us at the great bend in the river when some renegade whites destroyed his village. He was the only one left alive. Parker brought him home to me, as we could not have our own children. We have loved him ever since and have never hidden anything from him about his beginning. He knows he is a Kiowa Indian, like you."

Parker Cartbridge, aware of many sensations and feelings, said to Eagle One-claw, "Do I know why you have lived alone all these years in the mountains close by?"

Eagle One-claw, old as the hills, old as time as Roy phrased it in his mind, replied with an honest response. "For long time I know you know things Kiowa know. You kind to papoose for many years. Both of you." He nodded to Parker and Cybil Cartbridge as Roy Cartbridge began to feel again the fuzzy sensation sitting inside him, making way on him.

"We have done what we could," Cybil said, "and it's been a good job and a task we loved. He is a much loved boy." One hand touched the arm of Roy sitting beside her at the table. "He is a good Indian boy, of that you can be assured."

"Do you have robe he was found in?" Eagle One-claw said.

Cybil, letting go of the only secret they had kept from Roy, said, "Yes. I have kept it aside all these years."

She left the room, as Roy's mouth hung open in surprise. When she returned, she was carrying the buckskin robe in which Roy was brought to her the many years ago. She handed it to Eagle One-claw as Roy Cartbridge looked at his first robe with complete surprise.

Eagle One-claw held it up, then showed it to Roy Cartbridge. "I give you name on first day. Bear-with-Wings. You take new name when you grow up, like now."

"Why Bear-with-Wings?" Roy said.

"Only bear with wings could escape our rock pile. Only bear with wings could fly up on the mountain and laugh at us. All Kiowa know about bear with wings. What name will you take now?" He

67

handed the infant's robe to Roy Cartbridge. "I make the robe for you. I am grandfather to Bear-with-Wings."

"I will be Bear-with-Wings again," Roy said, "Bear-with-Wings, Kiowa. I will spend the winter with you in the mountains and you will teach me the Kiowa ways."

Cybil Cartbridge, knowing the letting-go time had come, nodded her agreement.

The two Indians, grandfather and grandson, separated only by a short distance for the long years, knew the bonding as it began in earnest, as the young man's mother and father looked on, as the legend of Bear-with-Wings began circulating once more.

The Shoshoni Sheriff

For a long time Jimmy Ditson nursed a deep desire to become sheriff of Sunquit. It sat in him like a tree had taken root, socked down deep, making way. Behind it was a love of the land that did not need to be nurtured: rather, providentially, that love had been in him since the beginning and that love continued to flourish. He was only 18 years old at election time but every knowledgeable person in Sunquit knew he was the best rider, the best roper and, most important, the best shooter in the whole Snake River region. He'd be the best sheriff, of course. Hadn't he by himself faced up and beaten off five rustlers who wanted a piece of his father's herd, had driven them clean across the valley and up along the river like a banshee was chasing them? Nobody ever heard from them again, the way stories eventually come back to their point of origin, the way crooks somehow have to come back to the scene of the crime.

It looked like a cinch that he was going to get the job because nobody was actually running against him except an old town flannel-mouth looking for free drinks and long conversation. That's when an old ranch hand of his father, Ginger Clougherty, rickety, really slowed down, riding what might be his last horse, came loping back into town on an off-hand visit and mentioned that he thought Jimmy Ditson was really an Indian kid. He didn't say anymore, but the threat was there and the hackles began to rise in some quarters. Another town man threw his hat into the mix, tripling the options.

Talk about "The Shoshoni Sheriff" began to circulate. Of course, none of it was mentioned in front of Joe Ditson, Jimmy's father, a most respected rancher in the part and a great boss. But the word was out and about, as the barber would say. The word circulated throughout Sunquit, some people believing and some not as sides began to develop in the coming election. In saloon and barbershop the talk created arguments and, as often happens, out and out hostility.

"Who wants a damned Indian as sheriff?" a displaced Irishman yelled out. "He'd sell us out, any of them would," and another man answered, "Who the hell wouldn't blame them the way the government treats them like they were foreigners. There were here before us. Just like the Crown sent its soldiers into your old Ireland. Did you fight or run, Dolan?" His fists were doubled even as he spoke.

The fight was a major breakout, and Sunquit could feel itself breathing deep into the night.

When things cooled off from that fight, new talk started, and Ginger Clougherty jumped right back into it. "I heard up the line, from an army trooper, that one squaw is said to have left a baby someplace years ago, to get proper care while she was on the run from the army driving to get the Shoshonis onto the reservation. Nobody knows her name, but one buck said her name was White Flower Curled Over. It's just another story that a few drunk injuns keep talking about, like the kid is supposed to come back someday when the mother calls. Like he'd know her, huh?" He paused, as story tellers do, before he said, "Heard it was the Ditson place."

It all began about 18 years before.

Fifteen years married, childless the whole while, Grace and Joe Ditson felt the clock winding down on their chances to become parents. A local beauty with the warmest smile one could imagine, she was in her mid-thirties, and Joe, a bit older, was a rugged, dogged rancher who kept on the move. Handsome in a dark way, curried with a sense of joy at the world around him, nothing much escaped his eye or his attention. Along the Snake River the two were known as a hard-working and devoted couple whose ranch sat on a lovely piece of geography and folks in Sunquit, the nearest town a half day's ride down river, often talked about what a great place their ranch would be for a child to grow up on. It all changed the early September morning, mountain cooled air settling onto the lower landscape, the sun just breasting Putney Peak, that Joe went out of the ranch house to milk the cow. Grace, as she usually did right through to spring, turned up the collar of his jacket before he left the house. Ditson drew in a rich lungful of the dawn. On a ridge uphill from him, lit up by the rays of the sun, he saw a figure of indistinct form looking down on the ranch, and then apparently turned to walk away. The air was sieve of cold traces, and he knew a sensation of unknown origin, as though it was pummeling him awake.

That's when Joe Ditson, for the first time ever, heard a baby cry on his ranch, on Grace's ranch.

The first squall, from inside the barn, sent a chill across the back of his neck, even with the collar pushed tightly up under his Stetson. Before he dared hope for an unlikely gift, he could see Grace's smile blooming like a spring flower. As he rushed toward the barn, coolness still a valid sensation, he turned to look up the hill once more. A dot of the indistinct form disappeared over the brow of the hill, as though a quick goodbye had been said after a short visit.

In the barn, from somewhere deeply inside, hidden or covered, he heard the cry again. It came from a corner where a pile of hay sat as tall as he was. In the midst of the lower edge of the pile the baby was wrapped in warm hay, a warm deer hide, and cradled in a crude but strong basket. Ditson's rugged hand touched the soft, sweet and cool forehead of the child who had dark eyes, dark brows and a light blond tint in forelocks showing under a sleeve of a hat. The child looked up at him and smiled. The warmth almost choked Ditson on the spot, and then plunged down into his innards.

He picked up the basket, light as a bird's nest, brushed off the hay and rushed to the house, calling out Grace's name as he ran. "Heat up the stove, Gracie. Get some water going. There's a baby here, Gracie." His yells were loud, demanding, and full of surprise, and he was suddenly conscious that he had not called her Gracie in years.

Grace heard her husband's yells and then the baby cry, a whimper of a cry as the child bounced with her husband into the kitchen. Grace was, immediately, all hands and all action … another log on the fire, a pot of water moved to the front of the stove, her hands out to hold the newcomer, to make way her kind of welcome.

Her smile broke like a May morning on the meadows, and Joe Ditson almost melted again. The new warmth broke in behind his collar and melted again down through him.

In a demanding quiz she said, "Where? When? How?" Then, shrugging her shoulders, said, "Who?" asking the really important question. Grace asked the questions practically in one mouthful as she held the baby close. She suddenly stripped the skins off to find it was a baby boy. She said, her surprise and delight continuing, "I think he's about three months old," as if she had been a mother forever. A woolen blanket was wrapped tightly around him with a mother's caress.

"In the barn," Ditson said. "I saw someone on the top of the hill out past the front pasture, looking back this way. It could have been the mother. I am not sure. It could have been a Shoshoni woman. The baby was put in among the hay, warm, but easy to spot, like he was meant to be found quickly. The deer skin says she's Indian as far as I'm concerned. And the troops have been moving the Shoshonis around for months like they don't even belong here."

"If it is his mother, do you think she'll be back?" The child was hugged to her chest, the wide eyes looking at Ditson over Grace's shoulder. The smile continued radiant on her face. "He gets a bath as soon as the water's warm. Get that nursing rig you used on the lambs when the yew was killed by the wolf. And go milk the cow right away. He'll need fresh milk. You hurry, hon. I'll take care of him."

"What'll we call him?"

"James. Jim. Jimmy. Jimmy Ditson. Yes. His name is James from now on. You can call him what you want. For me he's Jimmy."

"Jimmy it'll be." Ditson went to milk the cow. He had a son, for the time being, and it felt as good as he always thought it would feel.

The boy grew well on the Ditson ranch, in the care of loving parents-at-will. The blond hair belied his mysterious appearance and the connection with what Grace and her husband always believed was a Shoshoni maiden either ousted from her tribe or driven by soldiers as part of the government decree. Either in private, or often in deep thought, they wondered about her coming back. Would it be threat or salvation, for them, for the boy, for his real mother?

Sometimes those thoughts disappeared in a wink as they reveled in Jimmy's growth and his inborn skills with rope, horse and rifle. A natural hunter he was, patient, skillful, and able to devise and react to situations met in the mountains and out on the vast plains. And he was a handsome young prince, as Grace often said, noting always the golden patch of hair that sat like a pompadour on the top of his brow.

The ranch hands, in a flux of arrival and departure, paid little attention to the youngster as he grew through the tiers of his years and the rounds of a changing of the guard, as it were. Most of the cowboys, herdsmen most of their adult life, worked hard and loyally while on the payroll, and played hard whenever they had a chance. Those opportunities came mostly down river at Sunquit. And they talked little, carried conversation in stories and escapades rather than in rumor.

Yet, Joe Ditson, no angel in his younger years, knew where most rumors were exchanged … at the bar, in a card game, or an upstairs room for rent on a Saturday night. He was fully aware that Jimmy's arrival would surface sometime down the road, or down river, as he corrected his own thought.

The threat of such revelation never bothered him much in the face of circumstances that he never once told Grace about, and which had accidently come to him ... not from town, but from the crown of the same hill where he thought he might have seen Jimmy's real mother. A frequency of it developed and he began to enter a log of marks on a beam in the barn.

One morning, in the heart of spring, the pasture alive with color of new blossoms, a breath of surprise in the air, Joe Ditson saw again a horseback rider on the brow of the same hill. Jimmy was helping to break in a few horses and was showing off his skill at it, and a lot of whooping was going on among a few ranch hands. "Way to go, kid," they said in unison. "You got him now. He's gonna remember you next time he grits his teeth. 'Member that, Jimmy, cause he'll remember you. They don't none forget their first ride or their best boss. That's horse talk for you, kid." They all laughed loudly and slapped hands, all of them thinking about Saturday night in Sunquit, half a day down the river, half way to hell or heaven.

Jimmy Ditson, they had agreed, was as dogged and determined as his father, and probably a better rider from the word go. They applauded again and laughed again at creative moves to stay in the saddle and his ordinary slight falls and thoroughly enjoyed the moment as though a shivaree was being shared.

And Ditson, the lone one among them noticing the distant visitor, played it casual, bringing no attention to the mysterious watcher.

That was when he made his next secret entry on the beam in the barn, *month-day-year* accompanied by a *V* for Visitor. He had done so for many years.

When Jimmy Ditson was 18 years old, and a party was to be celebrated for his approximate birthday, based on Grace's guess at his age the day he came to them in a basket in the barn, Ditson saw the frequency of visits had been firmly established. 16 times in the 18 years, just about one every year, in the summer, the rider had appeared, and the visit noted.

Ditson never rode out to investigate, because he'd always see Grace's collapse at the threat of losing her son. He assumed whoever it was was satisfied life had been decently good to the youngster. The repeated trips boded good interest, faithfulness and a sense of loyalty. In a strange way they made Ditson happy, because the visitor always made a point of being noticed, as if a message was being sent or delivered, or a love was being addressed.

But things going on in Sunquit about the election were brought to Ditson's attention. He would go in and see how things were going for Jimmy who had been in town for more than a week. He told Grace he had to go to Sunquit.

"I'm going in with you, Joe. No way am I staying here, out of the action. You get the rig and horses ready for a ride along the river and I'll get everything ready for the ride. Something to eat. Pack some clothes. It might be the first time he ever really needs us."

Her husband said, "Not counting that first time, Grace. You're the boy's mother, out and out. Nobody can say you're not." He headed out the door for the barn.

Grace, relaxed for a mere minute, remembered the first time she held the boy. It all came back to her and it was all worth it. She loved him with a passion she had never known, a mother's passion. She knew what it meant.

When Ditson brought the rig to the door, she was ready with clothes, food for the journey, and an ache in her heart that her boy might run into trouble. Jimmy had gone to town a week earlier where he had spent much time lately it seemed to her. It caused a smile she did not keep hidden from her husband.

For Jimmy the earlier ride into Sunquit was always the same for him, with the whole earth calling out to be noticed; the clutches of pine trees, the bunches of colorful flowers like checkerboards on the plains, the ridges so clearly defined in cliff faces they were like pages in a book and he knew he was being taught, that learning never ends even if you stop looking because you just start to hear it or smell it and you're right back where you started, looking at it from an anthill to a mountain top and the sun kissing that mountain top like a girl kisses her lover in morning's realization. Life, he knew, sparkled from that realization; he'd seen that from his parents.

Out beyond, in the wide-spread grass running to horizons, the prairie dogs called out. Overhead the hawks shifted their wings or trimmed their feathers onto new thermal edges and he swore he could read their eyes like a language spoken to him long ago, perhaps something his father had said in the shade of the barn or on the porch at night with fireflies for hovering company, or in the darkness of his room when covers were tucked in around him and the moon sat in his window like a Christmas present waiting to be opened.

Out there, beyond the hand-reach of growing things, the cholla cactus and the Devil's Claw had made deep footholds in wide swaths of landscape, like signposts had been erected for him and those who thought the way he did and rode the same road he did. Interpretation meant survival; he could feel it.

Sub-vocal speech pounded at him as he rode along, the river at times like a sheet unwinding from a huge roller, and catching the sun in so many angles he allowed that he could at times be blinded by their beauty and brightness. He wondered if he really wanted to be sheriff, and the earth gave him the answer, as it had always answered his many questions. So much was right on the earth that everything he could do to keep it that way was his responsibility. The lime hue of mesquite wrapped around his eyes and lingered there as if it wanted to be tasted, like a summer quench of aide on the porch at home on a hot day keeps punching at you without mercy until you know lime at the back of your throat for the balance of the day.

As usual the river kept calling for attention. Ripples. Animal or fish movement. Glancing sunlight like a mirror had been struck. The odor of rank-smelling arrow weed crawled to him from the near bank of the river. The dense thickets lined the river and smaller stream beds that marched overland to reach that long rush to the Gulf of Mexico. Much earlier he had determined that arrow weed stems were used for arrow shafts by local Indians. That came at him as another lesson in the classroom of the earth, and he was able to interpret the teachings that came to him: never close your senses to what is sent your way from the earth itself. Don't bite the hand that feeds you.

The ride of his parents was just as quiet most of the way. They finally loosened up from inner grasps, freeing their thoughts, as a few riders on horseback said hello and passed on ahead of them, obviously going in for the voting and what the weekend would bring to the celebration. Ditson had carriage blankets and oats onto the rig, and a rifle and ammo boxes sat at his feet. Grace paid no attention to the arms, though she realized that her husband was almost as good a shot as their son. It had taken him a few years practice to catch up to the boy who was a natural at everything he tried. An absolute natural who presumed survival. She could taste it. Long ago she had accepted his Indian blood as responsible for many of his talents, for his alertness, for his own sense of survival and that which he found himself responsible for. He never told her in words, but she saw it, as open as a page in a book.

A distant neighbor, from father up the river, caught up to them, after hailing them from a distance. "Hey, Joe, Grace, I guess we're all heading into town to make our vote. I'll vote for Jimmy. He's a sure fire winner. Catch up to me at the hotel, I'm getting thirsty. Been on the road all day. My son Paulie went in yesterday, Bobby's coming in the morning. They're all excited. I heard we're having some kind of fireworks when it's all tallied. I can't wait. See you there." He tipped his hat to Grace and was off down the road.

From the river came three shots as they rounded a bend in the road. Other neighbors, on two boats and a raft tied together, were floating down to Sunquit and hailed them with saluting gunfire. "See you in town, folks," they yelled out. "Good luck to the winner."

Grace said, "Oh, Joe, I hope he doesn't lose and I hope he doesn't win." She grabbed his arm and hugged him. "We've got to be ready."

Puzzled for a moment, Ditson said, "For what, Grace?"

"You know as well as I do, Joe. It won't be easy for him. People are funny with things like that, especially those who've lost family in the Indian affairs."

He nodded, understanding that he had again not fooled her one bit.

That afternoon, later, with a cluster of clouds darkening the sky but no rain expected, all kinds of hell broke loose in Sunquit.

When the sun broke through a cleft in the clouds, its slanted rays almost like a beamed flash down a tunnel, a Shoshoni Indian woman rode into town, right down the main street of Sunquit, past the bank and the saloon and the general store where a cluster of people stood gawk-eyed staring at her and her horse and her raiment, a cluster of beads and leather thongs and small strips of shiny metal draping the front of her deerskin dress. With a slow and deliberate movement, she dropped her reins in front of the sheriff's office. Regal looking, possibly a princess in the tribe, she sat so erect in the saddle people might think she was strapped to a board.

The outgoing sheriff rushed outside when he heard people yelling, a raucous screaming of threats and curses not heard in a while.

"Get her out of town, sheriff. She's trying to win the election for the Shoshoni sheriff waiting to get elected. It's all rigged. They're going to take our town away from us. They've been waiting to get it back."

"Easy, now, folks. Let's see what she has to say. Don't guess at what might have brought her here."

"String her up like they did a few years ago to the whole McWilliams family. Even the kids. Hang her right here. I'll get the rope."

Jimmy Ditson, lingering on the edges, became Johnny on the spot, moving to the front of the crowd and saying to the blabber mouth, "You going to put the noose around her neck, Lugo? You going to slap the rump of your own horse to kill a woman?"

"Easy, new, easy, now," said the sheriff again, his hand resting nervously on his holster.

"What have you got to say, lady? Who are you?"

The queenly-looking woman looked around and pointed at two men, a rancher who had come into town for the voting, and his foreman, a big hulking man.

"Ask them," she said, her hand pointing yet at the two men.

"Why the hell ask us?" both men said almost at once.

"Because 18 years ago, when I was just 14 years old, I was raped in my own bed on the ranch and ran away because I was so ashamed. The Shoshonis took me in and raised me. I was woman to Maken'towa'ttapph, a great leader, and he let me keep the child that was in me. He was good to me, more a father than a husband."

The rancher, seeking recognition, feeling the soul rise out of his body, remembering all the pain of a missing daughter, a runaway or victim of kidnapping, found something in her eyes. It was like looking at into his wife's eyes, her a long time dead from the pain of a lost child.

"Is that you, Esmie?" He was crying as he walked towards her, but even then he could not put his arms out to touch her.

The big, hulking man, the foreman, tried to slip away in the crowd.

"Stop him," she said. "He was the one who raped me, in my own bed. He is the father of the boy I left on the ranch with the good people, the people who have raised him, the one they call Jimmy Ditson.

It all came apart for many people, the long-time adopting parents, the boy who became a man, the girl's father, the man who

77

raped her in her own bed, the town of Sunquit.

The rapist, trying to run away, was shot by the girl's father, even as the dead man's son and the shooter's grandson looked on, before he, possibly the new sheriff, could get his gun out of his own holster.

Jimmy Ditson walked to the Indian woman. "My mother? Are you my real mother?" He looked over his shoulder at the Ditsons standing in the crowd. They were as silent as the crowd had become, a taste of loss in their mouths, a tug beginning its deep pull at their heartstrings.

"Yes. When you were a baby in the basket papoose I had a dream about you as a young man and I called you *He Who Walks on Warm Water*. In Shoshoni language, in *Sosoni' daigwapeha*, it's said *'Udenhakki-ba'I'mi'qwa baaquyu'wai'I'*. And I am called *Dosa'hepinkepph'maaqwandbuubi'ba'anqu*, White Flower Bent Over, because I came with a child in me, this child who has become a man despite his real father."

In truth, she was addressing the crowd in the middle of Sunquit's main street. "He is the image of his adoptive father and my adoptive husband, this boy has become this man who wants to be your sheriff."

Later that memorable day in the town's history, when the badge was pinned on Jimmy Ditson's shirt, the talk about "a Shoshoni Sheriff " gone like mist under sun, his two mothers were there, his adoptive father, his grandfather, and the whole town of Sunquit, practically every man and woman in the town limits.

A week later, Grace and Joe Ditson headed home after the swearing-in ceremony and enjoying Jimmy hearing from his real mother the quick legends and histories she had learned from tribal elders. A natural story teller, she spoke half in Shoshoni and half in western American, charming her son who sat bright-eyed and attentive to every word.

Jimmy beamed hearing about Mogollons and Zunis and the basket-making Anasazi and how all the way back, much earlier in the history of the world, the early Indians had crossed the ice in the north from another world and came down along the great Snake River to find new homes. He knew he was an heir, in some part, to all of it.

And further along the road, as the Ditsons approached their ranch up along the Snake River, the ride comfortable, the sun touching them with its grace, the prairie flowers all abloom about them, their adopted son Jimmy Ditson the new sheriff of Sunquit, they both turned to look back at the crest of the hill behind them. Together they waved at the figure on the crest of the rise waving back to them before disappearing from sight.

White Boy, Indian Brave Charlie Two-Tents

I was Christopher Happs (white) when I was born and Charlie Two-Tents (Indian) now, this day, as I am about to be hanged. Life for me, as will be evident, was always hanging in the balance. Looking back on it now, from this late circumstance, that life turned on more accidents in one man's existence than the mind can apprehend fully. Accidents are the unaccounted moments and deeds, some in tandem and some in their singular overtures, where lives, not just a life, in this case being my own, are involved.

At this minute, high on an old, rugged, man-killing scaffold, I can look out and see most of the people gathered here from this town in Nevada, right on the simmering edge of the Rockies, a place called Hell's Target, so aptly named, and most of the people off the ranches that surround this corner of the territory. Come they have to watch me hang for a murder or murders that I did not commit. Here, as if on consignment in life, I have no reason to lie.

Let me tell you my story, beginning here on this ignoble parapet of wood from which I can see my beloved mountains most directly north of this town now called Hell's Target, but once was the village of Manatanka, great chief of the tribe. Then, in the days of that great chieftain, it was he who found a woman to teach me to read at a tender age. He had said to that woman, in great wisdom and revelation only the great souls can touch, "We found you in the mountains desperate for food and shelter, and a place, a good place, with the living. It was an accident we found you, for we were going to travel on another path and the way had been lit for us. The Great One Above, the One of Voices, at the moment of decision, said to me, 'Manatanka, are you sure you have chosen the right path?' His voice was the voice of the turtle at that moment, slow and sure of the words, for the turtle never hurries his words, weighing them as sure as a scale. I said back to The Great One Above, 'Your question has an answer folded within it, so I will let you give your sincere help here by a toss of a stone to select our path.' I summoned the white mother of this boy to my side, told her of my plight, and asked her to toss a stone of her choice in the air to determine our path by its fall. Of much wisdom was that woman, that mother, and she knew one course might help her and her son, and the other might do nothing. She studied a whole day on my plight, also having the patience of the turtle, and then pitched a stone, after all her thoughts and viewings of the land, down the path that lead us to you sitting alone, frightened, hungry, but not quite ready for the wolves or the coyotes or the ugly pigs. I saw you first before any of the tribe. I knew you were a gift from The Great One Above, for you were reading a book amid ruins and death scattered too far to measure. You said you were a teacher. I said I want you to teach this boy to read. He is a white boy claimed by us long ago. Here at my side is his mother who does not read, but who accidentally led us to you. But I want him to know both sides of his skin, both sides of his cloth, for he is both a white boy and has been since he first came to us Charlie Two-Tents, a Sioux of the Great Nations. We have taught him all a Sioux needs in this world; he can ride a horse to the sky and back, hunt the bear and the boar and the sheep and the deer and the great buffalo of the grass, fight any foe, track a shadow across open ground, know what berries and roots he can eat, how to treat hides and skins for best winter use, where the deepest dens are, where the snake waits to strike, how to save a leg or an arm broken by stone or wood or metal, and become a chief in his time."

That day my lessons started. All the words I know came from that single book at the beginning until I found a few in deserted cabins, once on a wagon of the dead, under a seat, as if it was to be given as a present at arrival somewhere along the trail or in the mountains. And I knew all the words in my teacher's mind. Her name was Miss Motherwell and we called her Voice of the Cave. She taught me for five years and Manatanka asked her one eventful day, after a great feast of buffalo meat, if she had done her job of teaching me to read and she replied, 'He knows more than I do.' So Manatanka gave her a horse and left her near a town well east of here and she went home to her own people, but cried leaving me, saying, 'Adieu, adieu, dear Charlie.' And I knew her meaning then, with the last word she taught me, and which I have not used yet.

But that was all in the beginning, at the very beginning, for I was barely into many years then, only about 10, and knew 'how to listen' as though it was the only rule in the world. I bit and chewed and tasted and swallowed every word she ever brought to me, first in my ear, and then on skin thin as the pages of the book. I knew it all at that tender age, and whenever Manatanka found a written thing, a book or page or poster or newspaper, he made me read it to him over and over again so that he could say it back to me from what he called the 'eye of his mind.' He kept saying 'I will not be second to the white man even in his own words. For the Great One Above told me that I dare not lose the advantage of what he had given to me.' He knew, before he died, the words of The White Father in Washington, who died just after Manatanka died and was left off the ground in a fire nearer to The Great One Above on the poles of two ash trees and two laurel trees and the skin of a bear three times his own size that he had killed by his own hand.

Manatanka said I was second in line for his high place, after Lion's Flight, but Lion's Flight was ever weary of my reading skills, and did not trust me. He said, 'White face does not disappear, but keeps coming.' Of course, he was right, for the white people, my first people, came on in relentless fashion, against my taken people, the gallant Sioux of the Great Nations, who will contest to the last warrior the taking of their mountains, their lands, by the people from overland.

All that departs, of course, from this current predicament of mine, where I can observe all the citizens of Hell's Target. And but minutes ago the under-swelling started from the crowd, where one man, with a loud and disturbing voice, in a crazy derby of some kind that few people wear out this way, kept screaming, "Hurry it up, will you, and get that damned Indian stretched by the neck. We ain't got all day here. Poker's waiting. My throat is dry. Don't cha know today's Satiday." With fancy footwork he danced a dance calling on decent energy, and some bodily control not all cowboys have. I guessed him a card player at his living.

Joining up with him were many disgruntled voices, another man saying, just as loud but with his arms waving and his hat waving like he was saluting me in my place, "Injuns ain't got the right to be treated this square. Not like us. Should have been hung on a tree out there at the McKenney place after we asked him where Nellie Mabel was. I bet you all agree with me, don't cha?"

Nelly Mabel was 13 years old, pretty but slow for her age, who often appeared at the edge of her parents' ranch where she fished in a small stream, never catching any fish that I ever saw, for I had seen her a number of times and even talked with her. In dresses so pretty you could see her for miles, ones that her mother made especially for her, she'd come along the path to the stream, always with a silly song coming from her mouth that she repeated a hundred times, but that silly song kept a smile on her face all the time. She was convinced that fish took on the squiggles of the worms she fed them. I had talked with her, but briefly, on the day she disappeared, which was the same day her parents were killed and the house robbed. One of the ranch hands had seen me talking with Nelly Mabel when he came back from town and found the parents dead. When he went to look for her, and me I suppose, we were not to be found. I was back up in the hills by that time and had no idea where Nelly Mabel was. I did later on, after I heard about the discoveries, find some current tracks near the stream, those of a few horses, and assumed that the killers realized Nelly Mabel had seen them and was a witness to murder.

If they took her, kidnapped her or visited harm upon her poor soul, she now without parents, I could give no accounting, for before I could trail the horses that left their tracks, I was arrested by the sheriff and his posse and brought here. The trial was over in an hour, and I am now condemned to hang.

All this time I have thought about the poor girl, slow enough, about to be tossed to the wolves of this mad town, her parents unable to protect her, no brothers or kin on the horizon to stand for her. No more will she be allowed to fish and sing her silly song, or enjoy the golden air, or the flowers beside the stream that so often matched her dresses. It was very evident that her mother paid attention to the flowers on the prairie and along the fishing stream.

More noise comes from the crowd, more yelling and impatience, and wanting to get on with the day in Hell's Target, and from afar I see the disruption on the fringes of the crowd as a man in a black eye-mask makes his way here to this scaffold, down the main street he comes between the bank and the barbershop on one side and the general store and the freighter directly across. People part at the edges, and the insertion moves like an arrow through the crowd, the way a chieftain might make his way, both with obligation and dominance. Noise ceases for a moment, and commotion ensues; probably questions as to his identity, for that identity must be sworn to secrecy, so that wearing such a mask does the job. He is, I fear, the hangman come to do his bidding. On a golden palomino he comes, a robust animal the sun lights up, and he wears a black crowned hat, black vest over a black shirt and denim trousers the land yet has a grip on. Easily he rides the proud horse, a gallant looking animal, and I am a good judge of gallant animals, having bred and run my own prairie horses, from wild stages right through birth of their young, growing colts with knobby legs, but full of promise. The Anasazi from old told us first of the magnificent animals that the Conqueror brought to this land from a far place, and in the matter of the fate of a man, one such horse carries my executioner to my feet to stretch my neck, as they have vouched in Hell's Target.

As I look about not one Sioux from the tribe is here, for would they not also be brought up here to share my fate? Of course, the way this small town runs on the food of frenzy and fear and unknown facts says it is so. I have no friends here, now that Nelly Mabel is away someplace, that quiet child though full of song, but only the one song. And this man, this hangman, who comes to do a job, will never know what kind of a man that I really am. That I killed my first puma at such an early age, and captured my white stallion in a canyon full of the sounds of terror. And he will not even know that I am able to read anything that he can read, and perhaps more. If I tell him of that ability, he will most likely laugh at a last ruse on my part to find mercy, as would the sheriff. But I have never cried. Not once in my life have I cried. I do not know my own tears, though I have seen others' tears, how they make their way slowly from the harbor of their eyes, the dam of their expression.

Never, I say again, has this white boy turned Sioux managed a tear from his eyes; not in battle, not in death, not at wounds of the body or of the soul.

But this man, this hangman, this stolid executioner, does not come pompous. He does not wear his vestments the way some of the lawmen do that hold sway in the region. Slowly he moves, patient, making no circus of his deed. He must value life, this hangman, in the most obvious conflict of deed and duty.

And as I look early down upon him, I am caused to lift my eyes and there lies my mountains rising against the great sky, green and white and fiery red and orange in a sunset, with the red slashes in steep stone faces, and the lines of ridges showing where the trails and paths are secret to the Sioux and the black mouths of the caves where some of the gods take to rest, where I chased my puma and met my maiden and high above, past the tree lines I see the snow lines where the sheep have tried in vain to hide from my arrows.

At this time, as the hangman rises slowly and somberly up the steps to reach me, I am visited by memories borne upon the mountains so sweet and so swift they rush through me like the wind in a long cave, and the sound of music comes along as that wind and quick breath cuts off corners like erosion itself is taking place at my ear.

His eyes are sad eyes as he looks at me. They peer out from the slits in his black mask, so blue I think of a tarn up high on the mountain where I swam as a boy with Red Eagle and Chosen Hand who have gone on long before me in the wars. A bit of hair sits on his face and on his chin, some of it gray and some brown as yet, and the sadness also sits at the corners of his mouth where those lips say sadness is about us this day, as if he makes somber announcements at his tasks.

No hatred fills me about him or his task, but only the hurrying sense of innocence that rushes through me trying to be found, but I cannot cry it out or shed tears to gain an edge for my innocence. His shirt is neat. He wears no badge or sign of status, nothing to say what he is, what he has come to do. But only the sadness in his eyes.

"Son," he says to me, lightly, almost a whisper, "I don't have any hate for you or any Indian that does me no harm, though I have been subject to great pain in my past. I have forgiven all things done unto me and onto mine. I don't know if you did the deed or deeds they have said came of your hands, for I am not a judge. I only come to finish the works of a trial. It is the way we do our things. The Sioux way is different, I have heard. Many of us admire your stand, how you fight for your land." He shook his head, looked at me again, and said, "It is the way we do things. That's all."

Then in an almost silent gesture, a bare whisper, he slipped a prairie flower inside my shirt and said, "I have brought you a part of the great grass, to carry with you, to know the odor of the plains.

His face was close to mine, his eyes intense but sad, trying to say all the things his heart carried.

I too whispered, in my turn. "I bear you no hate, sir. None at all. No hate. No sympathy. The way of the Sioux is different, we both know that. All is written in the Great Book, which I have read, at the suggestion of Manatanka."

He dropped his eyes from my eyes, and stepped behind me to slip the rope over my head. "Do you want a cover for your eyes?" he said, in a voice so courteous, so solicitous, so profound, it made me shake in my moccasins, thinking it too was the voice of The Great One in another body.

"No," I said. "One up here is sufficient." The very moment I uttered those words, I was sorry I had said them. I truly felt no hatred to this man.

Behind me, he attempted to fix my collar, the collar of my blue shirt, an old army shirt from the wars, a minie ball hole now soft in it, the sleeves holding stitching remnants of a soldier's rank, the blue severely faded, like the blue of a high noon sky over miles of a great plain of grass.

Suddenly, in a thunder of the fates that portend cataclysms and surprises, of lives at immediate change, the God of the Great Voice was at it again. I heard this hangman, this hidden man, this man behind a mask, speak to him of the Great Voice. "My god," he said. "What is this? What is this? Oh, God, what is this?"

It made me think the hangman was going to fall down dead, not me the selected one, up here on this pedestal they call the gallows.

He clasped me from behind, squeezing me with some inordinate pressure bearing on all my bones, on the cavity of my chest. My breath, near all of it, rushed elsewhere.

Then this hangman stepped around me and yelled down to the sheriff, his voice coming again from the great sky above, "Bill, Bill, this is Christopher. This is my son stolen from us many years ago. He has the mark on his neck, the same mark you first noticed. Come up here and look at it, Bill, this is my son, Christopher Happs. Christopher Happs." He hugged me again.

The sheriff rushed up the steps and grabbed the neck of my shirt, even as a buzz started sweeping the crowd. Then his arms encircled me. I heard his sobs too, deep and convulsive, like the sobs of the hangman. From far off I heard Miss Motherwell say, in a favored poem, "The angel comes never at once but all ways."

Silence sat in Hell's Target like it had never sat before. And way out on the edge of that silence, coming from some path of private wandering, I saw a girl moving slowly, deliberately, in a dress as pretty as a bouquet of prairie flowers, her hand in the hand of an elderly woman leading her from some lost place no one else knows.

Speedwing, Legend in the Making

A few Blackfoot tribal members said, joking or not but in all awareness of numbers, that Speedwing was half Indian, half white and half bird. The elders of the tribe laughed at this description, but held off on their decision on accepting his name as his final name, "to carry into history."

"Speedwing" had called out the name as a child, pronouncing the word so that many tribesmen nearby heard the name as plain as could be spoken, with the falcon streaking across the sky so often in discussions of the name that such testimony was added to the legend in the making, the falcon coming with the speed of lightning to make note of the name, the event, and the on-going relationship between bird and man.

Many of the tribe thought there could be no higher sign.

Speedwing's mother was a white girl, found on the prairie as a baby by a Blackfoot war party and brought back as a living trophy. A council sat to decide where the white baby was to be lodged and many supplicants spoke at the council. Some of them were childless women, some were rising from their own sadness or loss because a son or husband had been lost in battle or a child of their own taken by river or bear. And some squaws among them needed additional motivation in raising young members of the tribe. The supplicants all pleaded their cases and the length of the pleas caused doubt to swim in the council until an older squaw, childless herself but without self-pity, made a strong case for her selection.

Her name was Blue Feather and she came into the council as a "lost" person in the tribe because she was alone in her tipi and had survived on her wiles and capabilities learned over a long and hard life. Her husband long past, Hawk's Talon, had been a grand warrior but fell ill and died of an unknown cause in the dead of night, leaving Blue Feather alone. But this day her voice carried an aura in it, a sense of creation. There was not a single note of sadness or self-pity or a plea to fill out her empty life. More, there was an awareness rising in the council when she began to speak, as if some other power, a power from a different place, had been inserted into the council lodge.

Blue Feather, speaking with a solemn but not conciliatory voice, said, "I do not ask. I do not beg. I only tell you that this moment brings the beginning of a legend that will make the Blackfoot tribe more honored than ever among all the nations for the change that will come upon the land, from here to the far waters, from here to the heavy snows that lie long on the land, from here to the warm waters rushing upon the land. It has been told to me that this child, this lost baby yet mourned by some mother, when raised among us as a Blackfoot shall give our people a hero for all time to come, that his name will go with the wind from the mountains and the wind of the prairies as if his name had become part of the wind itself. This has been told to me from the holiest of caves in the holiest of mountains where Blackfoot legends have their beginnings."

She stopped talking and looked down upon the baby girl, in the center of the council, sleeping on a soft deerskin. Across Blue Feather's face came such a look of wonder and a further revelation within the council that she could not be denied. The council presented her the child to keep in her tipi, to raise as a Blackfoot, to fulfill the legend already in ascension about them. The wisest among them saw all this as the beginning of a truth.

Blue Feather, before she died, saw the child reared as a Blackfoot maiden and choose her final name as Bird-Mother after she gave birth to a son fathered by a Blackfoot warrior, Sun Eagle.

The legend, advanced beyond promise, had come to its real beginning.

Bird-Mother, watching her son grow, saw him become a swift runner as a boy and develop into a splendid athlete adept in many endeavors. But becoming an extraordinary runner was his fated promise. Many descriptions and testaments of his running ability entered directly into campfire discussions, and that is how a legend shares itself with truth and reality, how it becomes fact before the fiction wears itself out.

Now and then, in these campfire talks, a speaker would offer a new token of belief; "Even the dust he leaves behind him when he runs doesn't know it's been disturbed until he is long out of sight."

Wise heads would nod at that comment.

Another at a camp fire or a council meeting might add, "Nothing that moves on the land, not man or horse, can catch Speedwing unless he allows it. Even the turtle, though laughed at in any race he'd contemplate, has a special view on speed, and his voice is heard in the land, slow and steady in its way, for what the turtle is and not how the turtle moves."

Wise heads nodded at that statement also.

Word of Speedwing's prowess moved swiftly into all the tribes of the nations, including Gros Ventre, Assiniboine, Crow, Sioux, Shoshoni, Kalispel, Cheyenne, Nez Perce, and Couer d'Alene among others. Young braves ran with extra passion and they in turn carried the word about Speedwing. Now and then, on the open grass, young Indian boys would sprint out on their earnest contests and the word moved with them.

"In what manner will you carry out the settling of your name?" the chief elder of the Blackfoot tribe said, looking down from his enormous height into the eyes of Speedwing sitting at the final ceremony. The chief elder was an impressive looking man with his great height, muscular body, and his deep-set eyes that sat like dark moons above copper cheeks very pronounced in their setting. He was aware of Speedwing's deeds to date and found a distinct appreciation of where the young brave sat in the eyes of all the tribes, even as young as he was, and not yet severely tested in battle.

"I have thought of what to do to keep my name," Speedwing said. "I will one day run from the sunrise to the sunset without stopping to rest. This will be my legacy, that my name runs with me, that we will run from horizon to horizon faster than any Indian will ever run no matter what tribe or what nation sends him out to challenge us.

From then on, even as the stories grew, the tales became ponderous beside village campfires, and they called him Speedwing evermore, a Blackfoot brave with an honored name, honored in the tribe and honored by all the nations.

He grew taller than the average Blackfoot; in fact, almost as tall as the chief elder who was taller than all the Blackfoot braves; and he had hair the color of a midnight cave and wore much of it in braids that trailed out behind him when he ran from horizon to horizon. Just above his forehead his hair was shaped in a pompadour fashion touched with bear grease or a wet compound of clay and mud and allowed to dry in a selected shape. To Speedwing, as well as all the other braves in the tribe, hair was looked upon as spiritual and special and worn the same way. Only with shame or sadness upon them, like the death of a family member or a loss in a battle, would they cut their hair to show their feelings at the time.

At the same time, another story started rising to the west, in the land of the Coeur d'Alene tribe, where another young brave, having heard stories about Speedwing, trained with great determination to one day race against Speedwing. His name was Deer Floater or Deer-in-Wind, and he outran all the braves in his tribe, the "Schitsu'umsh," which means "the people living here" or "the discovered people," so identified by French fur traders a few hundred years earlier.

Speedwing, when he heard about the Coeur d'Alene rival, stood on the top of the mountain and called out his challenge: "Come run with me, Deer Floater, and we will burn the grass behind us, set the wild prairie on fire. The gods of the winds will be with us and we will run from dawn to dusk, from one horizon to the next. We are inheritors of the land, and the nations will speak of us forever as those who ran with the wind."

His words, relayed by messengers crossing the land, crossing the wide prairies and through the passes in the mountains, came to Deer Floater, and his reply set into further motion the great race that was to come: "I will race you anytime, Speedwing, so come here and we will have a great race and I will beat you in that race."

Of course, Speedwing was not to be put off by that message, and replied, "You are in no position to ask me to come to your land, and I will not presume to call you to this place where I have earned and learned my speed, but will meet you in a middle place, like the Valley of the Lonely Sun where we can run from horizon to horizon without interruption from a wild river or an unscalable mountain, or be deterred by the great buffalo herds. For the Valley of the Lost Sun is a place where the great buffalo herds have run away from, and with our race may we show to the great buffalo that it would again be a great and natural place to run with the wind, find the good grass at the end of a day's run, and sleep with a happy stomach.

"The return of the great buffalo herds to the Valley of the Lost Sun would be the finest thing that could happen to my people; it would be better than their having the best runner in all the nations. The young and the old cannot eat stories or tales of runners or races, cannot hold a memorial feast without a great meal of roast buffalo meat, and will never get fat on legends old or new. When the buffalo once roamed there they kept the people happy and comfortable. And also quizzical from the beginning, ever since the high gods sent them down to the first Blackfoot to set up a tipi on the wide grass of the world. Because tipis are covered with buffalo hides, the children often ask the elders what came first, the tipis or the buffalo, and are told they will learn the answer with long age."

Deer Floater was elated with the response and sent his agreement that the Valley of the Lonely Sun should be the place of the race. "Your wisdom runs with you, Speedwing," he said, "and the joy will be mine to contend with your speed, for I too hope to have wind at my back and in my lungs."

The two runners trained harder than ever in the two months before the great race, each one of them watched by many of their tribe, which included all their relatives. And new runners seemed to come from the training activity, as younger versions of the runners began to lick their chops at the great attention being delivered to the runners. The talk of the race and the contestants ranged far and wide, spreading to all nations on the land and, according to some, as far as word could go on the land before the great waters held it for their own out of jealousy.

So it was, according to Blackfoot history, the day of the great race came, and the Valley of the Lost Sun was a sudden host to a large audience of watchers scattered along the course, and in the foothills and on the higher parts of mountains. So many different headdresses were seen and so many different outfits of clothing worn that it appeared to be a meeting of all nations of the earth. There was plaited hair and mud-slicked hair and pompadour sweeps and tight high knots in hair and many of the gathering wore feathers situated in a vast variety of colors and sizes upon their heads, and they wore a great variety of clothing, as some wore breeches or loin clothes or saris or wraps of a hundred kind that it made some on-lookers believe the rainbow had landed in the Valley of the Lost Sun.

And the commotion caused a lot of talk between people interested in other hair customs and manners of dress and a good feeling prevailed among them.

And so the race began, at one point of the eastern horizon, where the sun rose from its sleep, at the meeting of two mountains broken by one trail, and it would end on the western horizon, where the sun went to bed, at the place where two rivers joined in a flood of waters rushing from wild mountains with white peaks.

The whole day would fall between the start and the finish of the race, and went as far as one could see from the highest point at start and finish.

Speedwing and Deer Floater showed hands in an old style, each hand upraised so that one hand was poised to present a gift and the other to accept a gift. This sent warmth throughout the gathering as they watched the runners standing perfectly upright in their starting places. The sun was yet a whisper, the wind a slight breath finding a target, and suddenly they heard a wolf call out from a high place, at which signal the race started.

They raced ahead of the wind, with the wind, for the wind, as the deer might float in a following wind, or a feather on the current. Along the route of the race the two runners were never far apart. And Speedwing knew he had a worthy opponent and Deer Floater realized the same. And song and chorus and huzzahs and cheers of every sort boomed out from the crowd and from the mountains and from the canyons that idled along the edge of the Valley of the Lost Sun, and from every critter who ought to have a part in the celebration of speed as fast as the wind. And with all that commotion there came a subtle and slow measure in the earth, a soft measure, as the earth began to tremble, so slightly at first it was barely noticeable, until, as if Mother Earth was preparing a new lesson for her students, knowledge began to slip into the mind of each Indian in the valley.

And there was a great rush come upon the land and reverberations and echoes and a thunder not heard in a long time and a violent shaking in the earth and over the crown of a low hill of grass, the long line of a slow rise across the whole of the Valley of the Lost Sun, came the suddenly remembered thunder in the ground under them, and one boy, never having heard the sound but remembering what his father had said it sounded like, cried out in a voice they say was heard at each end of the race, at the start of the race and at the finish of the race, "The buffalo are coming! The buffalo are coming!"

That huge herd seemingly without end, poured into the Valley of the Lost Sun completely unaware of all the gathering, as though they were not there.

And there was a feast of great proportions and new hides for old tipis and words of Blue Feather were remembered in all lodges and all the tipis: "I tell you that this moment brings the beginning of a legend that will make the Blackfoot tribe more honored than ever among all the nations for change that will come upon the land."

Herman Longburrow, Cherokee

Herman Longburrow, a flat-out 100 per cent Cherokee boy about nine years old, got his name from a German minister who rode a big black stallion, carried a bible for ready use when he came upon possible converts or those who wanted to pray, and a Colt on his right hip, generally hidden under his black coat in case a different statement was needed.

The minister, Rev. Klaus Werner of the Granted Grace Ministry, heard someone crying in a cave many hours after a swarm of army troops had set upon a Cherokee village. The youngster was frightened beyond his years for he had seen soldiers at work before ... unforgettable work. And the cave was a long, narrow confinement that might well have hidden a hundred others like him after other encounters. In the entire west, the burgeoning west, there had to be a place of comfort, a haven, for the boy. Klaus Werner would find it for him; fate, and the Good Lord, had decreed it.

The Good Lord had appointed the right man for the boy's salvation; the reverend was locked into that appointment as if the Good Lord had whispered it directly into his ear.

Rev. Werner was a reader of many sorts, the Good Book in one instance and the faces of people in another instance, in the mannerisms forecast by those people he came in contact with. He saw suspicion, cruelty, nervousness, keen awareness, fear of dangers of any kind, fear of the cloth from some people, and sundry other characteristics or traits that people carried visibly about on their countenances or in their body language.

He was rarely incorrect in his readings, or "the great suppositions that beat upon us in this life," as he'd often say.

And the Reverend Werner often made himself a target of a sermon, such as saying aloud, "I wonder what in heaven's sake I'll do with the young Indian. He's still frightened and doesn't know what's coming to him in this life, on top of what has already happened. If I can leave him someplace, not desert him so that he'd be left alone again, the Good Lord will send His graces this way."

The boy, even frightened, wore a sour face, and Werner couldn't blame him for that. Life was tough enough out in the growing west and he had an assortment of ideas of what the boy had been through before he came upon him. "There are so many curtains that separate us in our lifetimes," he said aloud as he tried to envision the future and his next sermon coming to any congregation he'd find.

The sun was at its high point, the heat coming heavy upon Werner in striking waves as he tapped his empty canteen and saw the haze of heat lift off the grass in a quick blanket of cloud-like vapor. His throat was coarse and dry. Not once had the boy asked for water, though Werner knew he had to be thirsty.

The pair of them came onto Conrad Dibbler's spread at the point furthest from the ranch house where Werner could see a single stone chimney poking into the far horizon.

Herman Longburrow's native clothing offered little covering but identified him as an Indian right up front. The two of them were not a couple of hundred yards onto the Dibbler spread, known as The Little CD, when a horseman came out of a small copse of trees and challenged them, waving a pistol in his hand.

"Whoa there, mister. Where you going? This is Little-CD land. No trespassing."

As Werner reached for the Good Book, in a small sack strung on his pommel, the rider aimed his pistol at him and said, "Easy there, mister. Pull your hand out slow. What you got there?"

As the rider asked his question, Werner marked his physical elements: he had big teeth in a large mouth that would be a huge smile if ever let go in a pleasant manner; bushy blond eyebrows meeting in the middle of his brow and making him serious looking; but in contradiction his Stetson sat back on his head in a casual, lackluster manner with no tie string visible saying he had no hard ride in front of him, as if he had all the answers before he asked his questions.

Holding up the Good Book, Werner said, "It's only the Good Book of the Lord, young man. The book of the Lord."

"I don't mean that book, mister. I mean him, that critter with no clothes hardly on him. That Indian critter who looks like he lost his way out here on the grass where he don't belong no how in the first place." The gun was still in his hand as he said, "He give you some trouble, did he?"

To himself, Werner said, "One more for me. Gent can't hide his feelings, not that he'd ever want to, I'd bet. Might shoot young Herman if I don't be careful here."

At the completion of his thoughts, he said to the cowpoke, "No

94

trouble from this youngster, Herman Longburrow, who has lost his mother and father and all his brothers and sisters to a rambunctious troop of soldiers who have more fear in them than the Indians have of the troops no matter how many there are nor where they are."

"Longburrow, huh? Hiding away was he? Where'd the Herman come from?"

The wise mouth was almost ready to break into a huge grin, when Werner said, "He got that name from me when I baptized him in the name of the Good Lord whose book I carry wherever I go. He's Herman Longburrow from now on in this here life, as declared by the Good Lord and me as his emissary."

Werner was still measuring the man.

"Well, my name is really my name, Clutch Harris, put on me by my mother and father. That's all. And I don't know what the boss will say about this, but you got to come with me and see him. Says anybody comes on his land he gets to know, see what they're up to, if you know what I mean. Now, let's get along there, you and the Injun, and head over that way toward the ranch."

Conrad Dibbler, a short man but wide in the shoulders and arms full of muscle, was throwing horseshoes directly in front of the ranch house, the shoes flung from his hands swinging in a gentle arc to clang in most attempts directly around or near an iron stake.

"Who've you got there, Clutch? I thought you'd be all alone out there today. Where'd you find the Injun kid, and who's that gent you got there who's all dressed up?"

Harris said, "The gent in black is a church man of some sort and the Injun was baptized by him as Herman Longburrow 'cause he found him hiding in a cave."

"What's your name, churchman? Mine's Conrad Dibbler and I own this spread and I don't want any Indians, baptized or not, on my place. Is that clear?" His chest puffed up as he spoke as if trying to impress Werner. "I carved this place out of nowhere, and I started with a horse and a shovel and an ax and nothing else."

Studying the rancher, Werner saw a contrived hero of sorts who, right from the start, tried to impress strangers with his history, his achievements. Werner had met all types and Dibbler was no different than others of the same ilk … self-important, contrived, seeking what they knew they'd never attain, real respect.

Werner said, "After all that, you're not going to offer us a drink of water on a hot day? That's mighty inhospitable of you, if I do say. All the Lord's children deserve water for their thirst. Are you saying different?"

"Well, Mister Whatever, I'm not worried about your feeling that way. It just ain't my way unless folks is just like me, and that kid ain't like me. No way."

"His people were here thousands of years before you, Mr. Dibbler, and they deserve a drink of water, no matter how they come here."

"You saying they come raiding me and I got to give them water. Hell, man, that ain't even fit to talk about."

Spinning about he said, "Clutch, you get them off here as quick as you can, and don't let 'em come back, the bigmouth with the collar or the Injun kid." He puffed his chest again and all of it was lost on Werner and Herman Longburrow who rode off with Harris.

"Out of hearing distance from Dibbler, going down an incline, Werner said, "Are you going to give us some water from your canteen, Clutch?"

"Hell, the boss'd run me off the place if I did. He ain't kidding any what he says."

"I'm not kidding when I tell you that Herman Longburrow's people will know you turned us down as well as your boss. Might not sit well with them. It wouldn't sit well with me if I were in their shoes. Makes me wonder if you spend a lot of your time out here alone, as a line rider or a fence rider and sleep in a line camp someplace all by yourself. I'm curious about that."

The air about them was thick with a promised fate, thick and hard to breathe, and harder to accept any of the consequences.

Harris's response was all body language at first, as though he was feeling an arrow out of nowhere or a hatchet flashing from evening shadows. The shiver was slight but perfectly visible to Werner.

"Well," said Harris, his whole demeanor changed by possibilities, "I been thirsty a time or two and it gets real touchy, so drink what you want and put the rest in your canteen. There's not much water between here and the Lucas ranch due west of us, against them mountains off there."

He pointed west. "Lucas'll be different from Dibbler and so will his wife. She's half Indian. Might even take to the boy herself.

They got no kids of their own."

The decree had come from close to the devil himself and Harris slipped back into a shell, realizing he had given up too much information to a complete stranger, no matter what kind of collar he had on.

And, as suggested or decreed, the Reverend Klaus Werner, and his protégé, Herman Longburrow, were welcomed at the Lucas ranch by both Harlow Lucas and his wife, half Cherokee herself and half white.

Werner had said, "I guess you'd like to have some comfort in your life, Ma'am." Mrs. Lucas's name had been Feather Drift early in life until she had been taken and raised by a family of settlers way out on the grass. It was her long-time hope that she'd be able to find some balance in her life, and that meant children.

"If you will take this boy off my hands, Ma'am, the Good Lord will bless you. I have no means to bring him along with me. He'd face continuous hostility in all the places where I'd go in my passage."

"I have no children of my own, Rev. Werner," she said, "and I will do my best for the boy as long as I have any breath in me. My husband will do as I suggest, for we both realize I have better sense than him. But he is a good man, a believer in the Good Lord, though he tends to be rash at times, like most men out here who struggle to survive."

Harlow Lucas and Feather Drift watched as Reverend Klaus Werner rode off on his big black stallion into his own destiny, their arms around Herman Longburrow, not yet ten years of age, not yet grown, not yet a college student, not yet a lawyer, not yet an advocate for the downtrodden, the lost, and those other youngsters dislocated from the Cherokee nation.

Michelle J. Foxx stood heroically as her ranch house burned to the ground, the barn ignited in three places, and her rifle aimed at Red-Dog Tongue sitting her own palomino he'd taken from the barn but minutes earlier. She knew she could kill him even as he smiled down at her, her husband off chasing a few horses the Indians had set free for that purpose by tossing a snake in among them. She saw Red-Dog Tongue widen his smile as she heard a sound behind her; death or worse was coming her way, so she fired and knocked the Cherokee clear off her favorite horse and heard another bullet shatter the edge of a post and tear through the Indian who crept behind her.

When she regained consciousness her husband's arms were holding her, the barn fires had been extinguished, and Red-Dog Tongue lie at her feet. The raiding party of about 30 had scattered at his death, heading back into the Freelet Hills strung the whole length of the river.

"Harley," she said, "I didn't think you'd get back and I wasn't going with him. Where'd you shoot from?"

"From the trench I started to dig for a new sump hole for trash. It got me close enough to get a shot at him and that's when I saw the one creeping up behind you. I picked him even as you started to aim at the chief." He hugged her and asked, "What do you think we should do now?"

Michelle knew he was asking her if they should leave the place and go elsewhere, start over, but it hit her in a different way. She saw the whole scenario at once and announced a fateful decision, "Here's what we should do," she said.

Harley Foxx was astounded at his wife's words, but swore he'd get it done as soon as she was comfortable. He put her in the barn, under cover and comfortable for the night, and went to work.

On the following morning Michelle, with a good night's rest, watched the scenario she had seen in a flash had put in place to bring the scene to completion.

Three small piles of wood, many yards apart, were covered with pine boughs in a rough triangle. In the middle of that triangle, on a framework six feet high of fence parts and boards taken from house remnants, rested the body of Red-Dog Tongue on a platform. All his personal ornaments were in view. They had been placed on a bright blanket Michelle had found in the barn.

As she had envisioned, she lit the first pile of wood and pine boughs on fire. At first the smoke rose slowly into the air of a very calm day, a day of no breezes. Soon the column rose as she had seen it, a steady and sure-enough signal for the whole tribal nation. The column of smoke rose like it was coming from the mouth of a kettle, and it went straight into the air. In innocence and ignorance of the meaning of such signals, she still waved a blanket at certain moments over the smoke issuing from the fire. The bundles of smoke also rose straight into the air.

Harley Foxx said, "They're up there, Michelle. I spotted a couple of them on the flat rock in the hills you can see just off to the right of the barn." Excitedly he added, "Now I see more of them. You've summoned them."

Michelle lit the second and the third piles of wood and pine boughs and the smoke of three fires rose, and when the small bundles of smoke rose also, she said, "Harley, those are bundles of words the whole nation will see. I hope they understand what we're up to."

Foxx said, "Michelle, I see hundreds of them now, and many of them are moving down to the little rise on the south end of the pasture."

With a determined stride she was on her horse and started out to the south pasture, after telling her husband to stay where he was. In a few moments she waved her hand in a sign of friendship and motioned with her hand for one rider to come forward. When a few started toward her, she raised one finger in the air. She waved it again, and a lone rider came along the wide grass. In her hand she held an unlit torch. As the Indian, a young brave came close to her, she lit the torch and held it out to him and pointed back over her shoulder, at Red-Dog Tongue easily visible on the framework, Indian style cremation.

The young brave she thought to be about 20 years of age took the torch from her hand, and said words in his language, words she could not hear but understood. The brave said the words a number of times, slid off his mount, approached the framework, looked at Red-Dog Tongue's emplacement, nodded, and said the same words again.

He lit the pile of wood beneath the framework with the torch, made a sweeping motion low over the ground, nodded once more at Michelle and Red-Dog Tongue, mounted his horse and left. He rode toward the south end of the pasture where hundreds of Cherokees sat their horses, and within minutes they were all out of sight.

A few days later, Foxx collected the ashes from the Indian style cremation in a bucket and placed them in a hole directly below where the framework ashes had been. Michelle placed a single piece of Red-Dog Tongue's possessions she had kept for one explicit purpose: placing his unstrung bow on the site.

Every night, from one full moon to the next full moon, an unseen Indian placed a small article at the site. No sound was ever heard by the Foxxes, no shadow or form seen, no other sign left to interpret.

For the 40 years of their life at the rebuilt ranch house, no other Indians ever trod the grounds where Michelle and Harley Foxx lived and where Red-Dog Tongue rested with the gods.

At Ease with Sgt. Able Startooth

Thunder and lightning pounded and slashed around the Teton peaks as though the gods were angry. Able Startooth, an Indian scout for army cavalry that had been dispatched to the area above the junction of the Uintah and Duchesne rivers in Utah when unrest among Ute Indians took place, watched from the secrecy of a cave as a half dozen Utes looked into the dark and lit skies. They jabbered among themselves. He did not have to hear their voices, knowing what they were saying, having no doubt about their concern; an angry god had come out of hiding, bent on making changes on the land.

He rode his horse as though they were one, used weapons as though he had invented them, and could run half the day and half the night, whichever came first. He had learned much already in his 29 years of life, and reading trail, body language and behavior of animals as well as men, had brought him along as a man comfortable with nature as well as with human interconnections. He knew himself readily comfortable in more than one world, in which his sharing was acceptable. The storm intrigued him, lightning, blasts of thunder roaring through canyons, millions of hidden stars waiting for new chances, a faithful moon beyond some dark hill cradling its glory, and ever, on the dawn of each day, after every storm, after this storm, the eternal sun that gathered all things unto itself, as set in place by the high god of the same sky the sun shared.

He had attracted people in his few years.

This new storm lasted less than an hour, though fierce it was. In the morning the sun came bright and cast itself across the land. Startooth studied the band of Utes, one of them obviously a leader, as they came from hiding where the storm and the night had driven them for haven. They talked and gesticulated and the leader finally used a stick to draw something in the ground that could not be yet dry. He spent enough time over a hand-drawn plot on the ground that Startooth assumed each one of the braves knew and understood the apparent instructions given to them. He believed the drawing scratched in the dirt was a map, and the talk was in support of some warring action yet to come.

Sgt. Startooth, a misfit to some people of his life, not yet where he belonged by passion and by need, was described by several cavalry officer in the Utah area as "one Indian who could track a dead possum through Hell if he had to, and was given such an order." Another sergeant of cavalry said, "I'd rather have him listening in the night than the damned possum playing games with us."

Startooth, a Shoshone, was aware of the gods that looked down on all people with an eye for correction and retribution where required. If the land itself, or the people who lived on it, needed change, were due for change, or had incited godly wrath, they'd better be aware of their apparent shortcomings. And he always remembered what his great father had said to him when he was being educated by the elders: "Coyotes and ants are the lead scouts for the animals in their coming back to take over their world again. Be aware of the signals. Never close your eyes or ears to them for you will know them when they get bountiful."

It took Startooth a long time to understand what his father and the other elders had said to him, realizing that they were warnings for the centuries.

With two trained pigeons, in a small cage he carried everywhere, Startooth came down to the site to study the map where the Ute leader had drawn directions in the earth. He easily spotted the designations for the fort and town at the edge of the Uintah River, three miles above the junction of the Uintah and Duchesne rivers. They'd attack in the morning for sure. He scratched the name of the town and fort on a piece of paper, along with a diagram of an arrow, tied it to the pigeon's leg and let it fly off. Then he sent a second pigeon as a safety measure, hoping a hawk would not take one of the pigeons in flight and the town and the fort personnel would be alerted in time.

His tribal friend and pigeon fancier and trainer, Two Paws, stood on guard for messages delivered by Startooth's pigeons. A few times they had been the difference in enemy attacks, which Startooth had determined beforehand from various sources, and used the pigeons to send the alarm. He did not expect any indebtedness or favors for his actions or abilities, but they did come to him.

Major Bantern had seen the value of Startooth' s pigeons and had promoted him to Scout Sergeant in the 9th Cavalry, in a detachment of black cavalry that had a decade-long history in the Wyoming region. He trusted the Shoshone with his own life.

And not far from the fort, in another attraction for Startooth, the widow Velma Browning, on a piece of land left by her husband, killed while fighting rustlers, knew Able Startooth was a special man. She had been living, and working the property for a half dozen years, her husband killed in 1879 and no man but hired help was ever allowed on the property. Startooth was the social exception, though visits were long months apart.

She was convinced fate had brought them into contact, knew the ease of it; he knew it to be the gods of the mountains and the wide grass.

But the twain had met, conversed, studied each other, found attractions, found the good ground in each other.

Now, with his pigeons sent aloft and his scouring the sky for the dreaded, swooping hawk or falcon bent on disrupting communications, Startooth thought about Velma being right in the path of the Utes. They were armed. They were aimed at the fort and local civilians holding sway on the land between them and the fort.

Urging his horse, he headed down the backside of the hill, hit the level ground just where the river made a wide curve, and let his mount go all out for Velma Browne's ranch. She was ahead of her time in many ways, and he hoped she had read the activities around her, and had taken to hiding where she had hid before, in a slim tunnel that went from under the ranch house to the well about 20 feet from the side of the house. Velma had shown him the layout. She explained how it worked, allowing someone from the house to go under the floor and move to the well where several rocks above water level and just below the surface were placed for easy removal. The climb out of the well was simple after that, with due caution of course on the part of the escapee.

Even as he rode, he tried to imagine the ways that she'd notice changes in the land. They had often talked about braves who were gathered for war sent messages that birds of the air and creatures on the ground sensed, read, were alerted to. Often those alerts were read by other creatures on the fringes of new activity.

With proper signs coming to her, he believed she'd have ordered her few hands to drive her herd, what there was of it, toward the fort. That way she'd know there was a chance for the hired hands and the cattle to be saved. In turn, she'd barricade herself in the house and be prepare to go underground if the ranch was overrun and her home threatened to be invaded.

"Woman of the grass is not afraid of dark under earth?"

Startooth had asked her after she'd explained the outlet. "She is not afraid of being buried before her real time of leaving?"

"No, Able," she had said, being the only one beside Major Bantern who called him Able. "I am not worried about that. I am as comfortable there as I am with you." She had no accompanying gesture until he held his hand out and signaled he understood her. In turn, Velma Browne placed a finger softly on his cheek. Twice she tapped him with that soft finger, knowing once again that he was the most handsome man she had ever known, his face chiseled and honed as keen as the finest arrow, the edges sharp and neat, yet as bold as the mountains themselves.

"Once," she had told herself, "I will tell him we have been paired from the beginning of all men and women." She often heard herself say the words in the same exact manner, with the same breath of truth in them.

The immediate transfer of her finger touch was spiritual, yet tangible, and he thought all she knew had kept her going in her hard times; she knew people who moved around her world, understood them, found strengths and weaknesses that other people did not see. A worthy woman she was, one who could be at home anyplace, on the grass, in the mountains, with her man. There was no doubt in his mind that Velma Browne would be the center, and the heart, of any abode she resided in regardless of how it was made, of logs or hides or the walls of a cave high in the Tetons. Knowledge of that order he had known for a long time.

Her face, in a manner of illumination, softened considerably when he was around, and enhanced her real beauty. Her hair was as golden as a prairie flower and her eyes made him think of a bird he had seen only once near the river, a small blue bird that only flew off when he reached his hand toward it on a low branch of a young tree hugging the banking. The bird, seemingly not startled, had risen gracefully from its perch and without the slightest strain of muscle was aloft. It made him think of Velma. From afar he had admired how she strode about the ranch, and yet he had seen immediately how her steps slowed when he was closer. Her move had alerted him right from the beginning and he was enthralled with her unsaid messages.

In her eyes he saw the new way for her, and its acceptance. It would be hard for her, and he knew the taunts that could and would come upon her. But he also found a resolve in her as strong as any woman he had ever known.

But no less a person than Bantern had professed the truth of the ground he was walking; "There will come torment, perhaps abuse, from her people; and you will be subject to the same thing, ridicule, spite, anger that seethes in one's soul, hatred for your personal gain, her fortune, her womanhood. I know of no two stronger people to face such odds than you and Mrs. Browne. Just be ever alert."

With such memories finding the way back into his mind, Startooth urged his horse for more speed and the pair ran up the side of the Uintah River, the morning sun in vivid reflection all along the surface of the river as far as the wide turn.

As he climbed one grade in a trail across the prairie, away from the bend in the river and toward Velma's ranch, he topped a quick mound, and saw across a further rise the massed Utes preparing to attack the ranch. From a past event in one of the 9th's battles, he estimated this force to be the same size as one the 9th had scattered in a Wyoming campaign, probably between 500 to 700 men, most of them on horseback. Those not on horseback were assigned to recapture and mount the horse of any brave killed in action or wounded too severely to ride. It was a tool of force constantly employed by good warriors … not to allow their forces to be reduced by lack of horses under control, saddled for war. Death, they knew, would come, and they had to be ready to fill the ranks, fill the break.

Startooth had seen Utes wage war, had seen them at their best and at their worst. Velma stood in line to be accursed of their anger and hatred, the land being changed by an angry god, leaving it to man to correct the change, if that was needed or demanded.

Leg-with-Wings, he knew, was the leader. He had met him a number of times in peaceful situations, but had heard of his battle prowess and subsequent activities in the wake of a victory; as he rode, those activities of Leg-with-Wings caused Startooth to fear deeply for Velma.

His horse, as if spurred by another force, plunged ahead as he hunted for words from his father, some words to handle the situation, give him honorable direction, yet weigh in on the problem with a solution, a resolve.

He heard his father say, "Courage of the turtle in his slow walk on the land is as high as bravery gets on the face of the earth, even as he moves slower than the flow of the beaver pond."

He saw the outcome, like pictures the ancients had scribed on the walls of canyons, on the faces of huge rocks, and as bold as some of the sculptures the Basque shepherds left on the flats of tree trunks.

Startooth's hand patted the neck of his horse, and the horse slowed from a mad rush to a slow gait, and then to an approach upon the Utes that equaled the turtle's flight. Some braves turned to see him coming when a scout issued an alert; the cry of a fox moved in among the braves ready for battle as Sgt. of Scouts Able Startooth came on them from the rear.

Startooth pointed, not at Leg-with-Wings but beyond him, to the suddenly-formed wall of army troops stretched in a wide line in front of Velma Browne's ranch. His hands talked to Leg-with-Wings in the old silent language of signs. He told Leg-with-Wings that many would be killed on both sides, that today was not a good day for fighting, and that Startooth's own chosen woman waited on him at the ranch.

The hands stopped talking and Leg-with-Wings said, "She is your woman, Startooth? The one who lives in wooden teepee? Who rides like brother wind and walks like brother breeze? She is your woman?"

Startooth nodded his answer and put his hand on his heart, his hand parallel to the ground, his thumb against his chest. Sergeant's stripes sat on his sleeves, but his hair sloped down in two thick braids, and his horse wore a saddle with Shoshone talk cut into the leather. The Ute chief saw all this.

Leg-with-Wings held up his hand in the sign of peace, a place in the massed braves opened, and Startooth walked through the space as he made the peace sign to Leg-with-Wings. Their eyes met, and Startooth said, "Deer Path waits for you in your teepee with the same promise I go to in the wooden teepee."

Major Bantern and Velma Browne, and the wall of troops, saw Startooth part the ranks of Ute braves, ride slowly toward them, with the Ute warriors moving away from their formation in the once-proposed battlefield.

Velma Browne rushed out to hold Startooth's hand as he rode through the line of troops, toward the ranch.

Relief flowed in all observers; deep expectations waited at the ranch for the new pair of lovers, Velma Browne, widow, leading Sgt. Able Startooth, army scout, by the hand into a new chapter of his life.

From a hidden spot uphill from a pool fed by the River of the Nations, Jobie Trask watched the Indian maiden as she swam in the cool-looking water, all the while perspiration cloaking him where he hunched down between two large rocks. He suspected her to be Cherokee, believed her to be beautiful, and had no idea at all that she was nude. None of those facts lined up in his thinking as he watched her swim with an elegant style from one end of the pool to the other end, perhaps 100 feet apart. He wondered if there were any fish in the water, or any big turtles. He shivered at the last thought and it made him stand by just in case she found trouble, or it found her … or so he told himself.

The pool was on the high end of the River of the Nations, at least a dozen miles from Sharpsville, and the abandoned fort there, in high Wyoming.

He thought he had seen her once before, near the gate of Fort Wilcox just before it was deserted by the 4th Cavalry Brigade heading off to unrest elsewhere, and just before he was put out of a job by the move. If she was the one he had seen, her name was Blue Wing. He recalled that a bit of mystery sat in her face that one time, in the natural rise of her cheekbones shaped by the slanting evening sun bidding goodbye to day, at lips that seemed to be tasting the very air, and in the dreamy, slow and subtle moves of a most curvaceous body.

Trask had been a scout for the brigade on a long assignment; his nine years in the territory had brought him invaluable knowledge of Indians, traders and hunters of the hills, and cattlemen of the range.

Trask was only 24 years old, looked 35 with weathered skin and carried the wary look of an older man in his eyes. Just under six feet tall, husky at chest and shoulders touting strength, he moved with confidence in each motion, having been "out and back" as his father had said enough times and the local sheriff had echoed those sentiments when he said, "He's been there and done most of it bound to be done." It was an accurate statement that many folks would agree on. When Trask walked into the Teton Hills Saloon all the customers counted him as countable on either side of an argument or a struggle. Two pistols were carried on his gun belt, he wore a magazine of new bullets like a badge on his shirt pocket, but unlike other western men, his feet were shod with a pair of highly-decorated leather boots made by a Cherokee friend. Trask explained the boots saying, "No Indian wears spurs and they've been riding horses longer than we have and I don't need spurs either."

He had friends all over the Nations, which included some Indian women. Yet he longingly looked at the maiden swimming in the blue pool, her dress on the bank and flattened in the sun, moccasins beside the dress, all with the sudden idea hitting him that she was naked down there in the water. For a bare moment he dwelled on that image, realized it was most likely true, and held his breath in expectation.

When a sudden movement caught his eye at the opposite end of the pool, not sure if it was a metallic flash or the white of a face amidst the green growth, he figured somebody else might be watching her too, from behind a clump of brush on another small rise. He closed one eye as he lined up the spot as if it was a target. In a new reflection off the sun, the top of a Stetson hat glowed pure white, and then a face followed it into his vision.

He knew it to be a kid from town, Clayton Shanks, a loner, maybe 15 or 16, touted as a harmless loser all the way and never employed for any length of time, and each of those occasions often shorter than a decent breath. Each time, Trask recalled, a girl was involved in the short stay. The sheriff and some people were aware Shanks might become a problem, and might someday hurt somebody. Yet some said he was a harmless and overgrown kid, like lard on a hook ... he'd become what he was meant to be.

Yet here he was spying on an Indian maiden who might be nude. There were many folks in town who'd say, "So what," to that, but here was trusty Jobie Trask doing the same damned thing as the kid Shanks.

Trask was sure that Blue Wing and Shanks had not spotted him or seen his horse tethered in a clutch of trees and brush behind a rugged outcropping. The whereabouts of Shanks' horse was unknown to Trask, perhaps hidden in another grove or in rocks behind the hill. It was sure he had not come on foot. But other doubts assailed Trask ... he could not shoot at Shanks for looking at a woman who might likely be nude at the time ... or close to it, he thought, as he again looked at the display of her clothing played out on the banking.

If he tried to get behind Shanks, the youngster might shoot at him, being this far out of town (perhaps he had already done something like it) or Blue Wing would see him also as a Peeping Tom, though his looking was accidental. The soft boots he wore, without spurs attached, might assure him of a close-up, face to face confrontation with Shanks.

No matter what he did, Blue Wing would see both of them as Peeping Toms; that bothered Trask.

And in the pool, with a graceful move, Blue Wing made a turn at the far end of the pool, her elegance visible to both pair of eyes.

The entire idyllic scene, a beautiful woman swimming nude in a pool of water, two men of sorts looking on and enjoying the display in a sensual setting, and a clear blue sky reflected in the pool's surface, was brought to a sudden change when two other men, mounted, came to the bank of the pool and ordered Blue Wing out of the pool.

"Over here, squaw," one of them said as he pointed to the pool's bank in front of him.

Blue Wing did not move as she crouched in the water at the lowest end of the pool. When the man fired a shot on the water near her, she started to swim back towards the pair of new strangers … and on the far end of the pool, from his place of hiding, Clayton Shanks bolted from his hiding place and ran for his horse.

One of the intruders yelled out, "Shoot that guy, Harry, and go after him. Make sure he's dead before you come back. He might be running for help, maybe for Injuns."

The mounted stranger rode off around the pool and went out of site, yelling out, "I'll get him, Jake. I'll get him, and you bet I'll be back. You better wait on me."

Blue Wing was in the middle of the pool, swimming slowly back, and the man named Harry yelled out to her, "That's the good old girl. You come over here where this old boy's gonna give you a big welcome."

He fired another shot close to her, and laughed as he did it, saying as she stroked again, "You know better don't you, woman? Now don't you?"

He fired again and Trask knew the man was drunk. It would be stupid to allow him another shot that might go crazy on him and hit Blue Wing.

Trask stood between the two rocks and put a round at the man's feet, right where he aimed it. Dust flew up around the man's ankles with chips of rock chattering and clattering in the air, and when he spun about to see who was shooting at him, he dropped his gun on the spot and raised his hands over his head.

"She's only a squaw woman, fella," he said in his partial stupor. "Just a squaw woman. What'er'ya shootin' at me for?" He stumbled as he spoke and let a look of amazement limp across his face.

Trask, in his harshest voice, said, "Jake, if you're not up on your horse and out of here in a minute, and without your gun, I'll kill you. Tell your pal Harry, if you ever catch up to him, if he hurts that kid who ran off, the whole town of Sharpsville will be after both of you. Better go now, pal. Part of your minute just got spent and I'm willing to keep talking if you want to hang around and listen."

The pool shooter was mounted and out of sight in a matter of a few minutes, dust swirling up from his hasty retreat, and Blue Wing was putting on her dress as Trask casually looked off downstream while she dressed.

But Jobie Trask had seen enough of Blue Wing to say that she was the most beautiful woman he had ever seen. He was hooked.

As she rode on the back of his mount, Blue Wing said, "Bad men were looking at Blue Wing when she swim in the pool. Were you looking at Blue Wing too when you shoot at man with gun shooting at water?"

Trask, feeling the loose coil of her against his back as they rode, her arms curling tightly around his waist, had difficulty in concentrating, so he answered her question with a barrage of questions of his own, each one offered as if in defense of his actions, especially his looking upon her as she swam alone in the pool.

"Why are you out here alone?"

"My horse run away on me when I pick wild flowers off grass."

"Why were you alone?"

"I make surprise for chief who is my father. His name is Red Horse Run."

"Why did your horse run off?"

"Snake make him run."

"How far is your village?"

"Take half day. Village in valley beyond rock place."

"Are there any flowers there?"

"Not like flowers grow in grass and sun many day."

"Will Chief Red Horse Run be angry at me for making Blue Wing ride on my horse with me?"

"Chief not be angry. He know what you do for me at pool."

"How will he know that?"

"Chief send Rain Mountain to watch me. Rain Mountain is brother of chief."

"Why didn't Rain Mountain do something when the bad men came and shoot near you? Is he your brave?"

"He old now, only watch to tell chief. I have no brave of my own. Not yet but may have soon."

Trask felt a slight squeezing where her arms coiled about his chest, and Blue Wing's words sank into him as if they were lodged to stay in a special chamber inside. The words made him fully alert to her physical charms, and the clean, new scent of the woman, shortly from a swim in a pool, whose newly wrapped arms became tighter it seemed with each stride of his horse.

"I think you good shooter. Is true?"

Her question surprised him. "Why do you ask that?"

"Chief who see daughter ride on horse with man, make sure man can shoot, man worthy of daughter, man protect daughter, man be brave as brave can be. Chief make him shoot better than other braves. Man need prove he good shooter."

A sudden awareness hit Trask. "Where is Rain Mountain now?"

"He follow us. Watch us. Go with us to village in the rocks, tell chief what happened to daughter."

She directed him into a pass he had never entered before, and he stared in amazement to see it break out into a small valley as green as it could be. He took a second look and saw no flowers growing in the small meadow, but at the far end many tipis coned into the air.

When Trask asked Blue Wing why there were no flowers, she said, "Daughter pick all for chief, surprise every day."

"He must be a great chief," Trask replied, looking again at the meadow with not a single flower growing on it.

"Great Chief Red Horse Run must be wise before brave. Must lead others even before battle, so must be wise, earn good and many surprises, some every day from daughter."

Trask, now that he had the opportunity, wanted to learn as much as he could about Indian chiefs, her father in particular.

"If Red Horse Run was a coward but wiser than all others, would he still be chief?"

Blue Wing had a strange look on her face when she heard Trask ask that question. "If he wise to start with," she said, "he know that others know him before he know himself, so he will not wear bonnet of chief ever if he is coward."

Though he was always alert on the trail, but was now engrossed with Blue Wing's beliefs, Trask failed to see the brave that appeared directly in front of him as if he had been spurred up by promise.

The brave, unusually tall and unusually impressive, was mounted bareback on a pinto pony and carried no visible weapon, and though smeared with facial and body war paint his attitude showed mostly in his dark face. His eyes were staring at Trask as if Trask was guilty of a horrendous crime against the Indian nations. Trask saw the body paint of the Indian leap like a flame across his chest, the way a night fire is seen by a far observer. Trask believed the Indian was a messenger of notice rather than a warrior about to do battle.

Trask said to Blue Wing, "I guess you know this fellow, don't you? Looks like he's got some kind of message about him. Do you know him, what he's about, what's next?"

"He is Tall Tree," Blue Wing responded. "Red Horse Run send him to bring us to him. He wears paint all the time. He hate white men take away land of the gods. He know since he was papoose he fight for land of the gods. He fight any man, but only when Red Horse Run tell him."

"So what's next? What happens now?" He was thinking a duel was in store for him.

"You will see when Red Horse Run tell Tale Tree what to do. Red Horse Run know about you and Blue Wing and two men at pool. I do not worry for you."

Tall Tree spoke in the language to Blue Wing and she led the way to the far end of the valley where one tipi was larger and stood taller than all the others. She walked alone to the tipi and entered, after more Indian talk from Tall Tree.

For several minutes Trask sat his mount in front of the big tipi and little attention was paid to him by Tall Tree or Indian women at different tasks. Some of them were grinding corn, some were preparing fish and some were cutting up large chunks of meat that younger girls carried off to several fires, where smoke began to swirl into the air. The aroma carried well to Trask who knew a quick hunger.

112

As Trask studied the area he did not see many braves around, except for Tall Tree and two others off to one side, appearing as if idle. He had not yet seen any weapons, not a single rifle or bow and arrow or spear or tomahawk. Yet there was meat that had been killed and butchered, fish that was had been caught, grain that had been harvested. And there was little if any movement around the two dozen or so tipis spread across that end of the valley.

It was an idyllic scene indeed, thought Trask, and then Blue Wing, as if in perfect accompaniment to it all, somehow as beautiful as the calm scene about him, came out if the tipi. She was followed by an Indian shorter than Tall Tree, wearing no war paint, carrying no weapon, who yet cast about him an imperial aura. "No doubt," Trask said under his breath, "this is Red Horse Run."

The chief came right to Trask's horse, patted the animal with a confident move, and said, "Welcome to my village. Please step down. Trask does honor to my daughter, to me, and to my village. A chief needs such honor for his daughter." His pause was specific, and pointed, as he swept his hand to include something larger than what was seen. "And to my whole tribe."

"That's a whole lot to chew on," Trask said to himself again as he dismounted in front of the chief, with hardly any of the tribe present.

Red Horse Run, after his illuminating pause, said to Trask, his eyes on him, "In her foolish way she wandered too far alone to gather prairie flowers and was at the mercy of strangers, and to you. You did her well and she speaks well of you. She says your eyes are eager for her, as her eyes are eager for you. Do you think she is telling the truth? Do your eyes tell the truth?" He folded his arms over his chest, in an imperial way, but his eyes were open and friendly.

Trask, conscious of Blue Wing standing by his side, aware of Red Horse Run's penetrating stare, said, "Both of us speak the truth." He believed at the moment he was at a point in his life that he would remember forever, and the thought settled in place with deep resolve.

With a nod, though not as imperial as before, the chief said, "Blue Wing and Rain Mountain tell me you are a good shooter. Can you protect Blue Wing forever with your shooting? Are you sure of your shooting?"

"Yes, I am," Trask vowed.

"You are best shooter you know?"

"Yes, I am," Trask affirmed.

The smile that crossed the chief's face was still pleasant, as he said, "We will test your truth. My daughter Blue Wing is not like frightened bird, does not leap too quick, but she is a woman and must also show her truth."

Red Horse Run yelled out in his language a string of words Trask could not begin to understand, but was aware of some intent in them, something important was due after all the talk of truth.

Several Indians appeared from nowhere, bringing a rig that looked like a tripod for a camera Trask had seen a writer use to take a photo, but this rig was made of stripped branches and stood in a clumsy way about five feet tall when opened. A small piece of wood, flat and square, was placed atop the three points protruding each at the same level above a knotted leather bind.

The chief spoke the language again and one brave placed a small melon on the top of the flat piece. Then Red Horse Run stepped off twenty paces, spun about, and said to Trask, "You stand here and shoot there and knock melon off wood and not move wood. Only try if you think you can shoot only the melon. Blue Wing will watch you."

Trask, not nervous at all, as confident as if a cloak was wrapped around him, stepped to the line drawn by the chief, pulled his pistol and shot the melon without disturbing the flat board.

Blue Wing smiled a wide smile that cut into Trask with deepest affection. The chief nodded, and made another command to the braves, and one of them put an apple on the board, an apple that was half the size of the melon, and the chief turned to Trask and said, "Trask shoot again with confidence?"

Trask understood the question, and stepped to the line, drew his weapon, aimed, and shot the core right out of the apple.

Again Blue Wing smiled and the chief nodded, and then he made a series of verbal deliveries in the language. One brave produced a nut much smaller than the apple, and took Blue Wing by the hand and stood her directly in front of the tripod. He placed the nut on the flat board that was just visible above the top of Blue Wing's head. And almost in some kind of mimicry, the brave, with his hands over his ears ran, off to hide behind a tipi.

Blue Wing smiled, Trask gulped, and Red Horse Run said, "If Trask can shoot nut off board, Trask can have Blue Wing forever."

At the line, Trask felt the sweat running down his back, down from his forehead onto his nose and then dripped off the end of his nose. He wiped his brow, looked at Blue Wing smiling at him, knew he'd love her forever, saw the imperial chief fold his arms across his chest as if the eternal gesture was at hand, and Trask drew his pistol from its holster.

He took aim, and Red Horse Run said, "Trask can stop shooting now. Only the great god of the mountain is perfect. Chief cannot ask Trask to be a perfect, to be god of the mountain, only to be a good man for daughter of Cherokee chief. I will make you married this day."

Blue Wing hugged Jobie Trask and whispered, "Will my husband this day take me back to the pool?"

Trask understood everything she meant.

Noted Indian hater Jed Cawley, owner of the J-Box-C spread, was the only rancher in the whole of Mildred's River Valley who had complained about missing cattle ... not rustled or stolen one way or another or eaten on the premises ... but missing cattle. Three times he had complained to Sheriff Tim Cassidy about "these situations going on around here. Sometimes I take a count and I'm down 40-50 head in a week. There's not much sign, so you know it's got to be injuns doing it."

"I admit," the sheriff replied, "that injuns are the only ones who can go through a place without leaving sign, them and the ghosts hanging around in the canyons."

"You don't believe that, do you? This stuff about ghosts, spirits, shamans near to God?"

"Well, we'll see," Cassidy said, as if it was the closing of the conversation. He stood abruptly, reaching for his sombrero.

"Yeh, we will," Cawley put into the air. The simple words hung as heavy as a threat.

That threat was revealed later in the day, dusk mingling on the horizon with tree lines and ridges, dust rolling on the road into town and across dry grass, when an excited young cowpoke entered Cassidy's office.

"Sheriff," said an out-of-breath Brace Crowell, flashing his hands in the air, raising his voice to match his excitement, "I'm telling you there's cows in that taboo canyon that belong to some of us. Lots of them. I counted 30-40 head and couldn't see around the whole canyon."

"You see any brands on them? What are they doing in there? Did you go in there, Brace?"

"Hell no, Sheriff. There's redskins in there cutting them up, like it's a butcher shop. I ain't about to mix in with them less'n I can help it. They look mean as all get-out."

"You count them injuns like you counted the cows?" Sheriff Cassidy said, a scowl beginning to set on his face.

"I'm not kidding around, Sheriff. This is no joke. "

"No brands you know of. No cattlemen complaining of 30 or 40 head lost, stolen, or plain missing. None of them injuns chase you out of there?"

"Jed Cawley says they're the Seven Bands of the Lakota Sioux. Says some call them the Tetons and meaner looking than Hell on fire."

"Think they might be hungry, Brace? Hungry enough to cut up some cattle been grazing on their land? You ever think about them being here so long, these Indians, here before any of us dropped a lasso in place or rode a horse or ran a cow or mustang to corral? Before any of us saddled up and giddy-upped?"

Crowell was nervous all over. "Why you asking me all these questions, Sheriff? I'm telling you what I saw. That's all."

"That's all is right, Brace. It ain't enough for me to go running and gunning up there with a passel a men to get killed if it's a fool errand."

"I'll go with you, Sheriff. I'd be a part of the posse."

"Sure you will, all the way to the end, won't you? So tell me straight out, Brace, who sent you here, and you lie to me once more and I'll slap you in a cell so fast you won't get to a dance for a month of Saturday nights. Maybe two or three month's worth." He stood up, pointed his finger at Crowell and said, "I can guarantee you that. Who was it?" He jabbed him again. The soft edges of the sheriff's eyes seemed whittled away by slow frustration and found a new hardness.

But it was just as Sheriff Cassidy figured ... Crowell melted under little pressure. "Cawley," he said, "Jed Cawley," as if it was a total release. "Said he'd whip me and feed me to Jepson's hogs if I didn't tell you just what he said and I already told you that."

The sheriff leaped in. "I'll tell you something once, Brace, 'cause you're young and got to learn. That's Seven Cave Canyon. It's a holy place. It was named by the Seven Bands of the Sioux. I been in there once and won't ever go back in. You best hear what I'm saying ... it ain't no place for us palefaces. That's a fact of life best learnt early."

"What happened in there, Sheriff? You get scared out of there?"

"Brace," the sheriff said, "don't be a dung-nosed sappy kid with too much sass. You're damned right I was scared. I was run off like a lonely doggie looking for his momma. Them Lakota or Blackfoot or Minnecojou or Two Kettles, no matter who's ever in there from the Nation, ain't ones to mess with on your best day. I've seen 'em work. I've seen 'em play. I've seen 'em fight like they ain't ever scared of dyin', no matter what it looks like comin' on 'em."

The missing cattle situation came up again in the Long Barrel Saloon that night as Cawley and Crowell stepped up to the bar and Cawley said to the barkeep and his loud aside to all who could hear, "Drinks for the house, Abe. That includes the sheriff over there at his favorite table, him resting at the end of a tough day."

He tipped his glass to the sheriff. "Won't you tell us why you're not going in there trying to get my cows back, cows that were stolen from me?"

Cassidy, somewhat expecting the whole routine, thus started and getting warmer, replied in a soft voice, "I'm not in a rilin' mood, Cawley. You and your little pigeon there," and he pointed his empty glass at Crowell already getting a little red in the face, "ain't told me one mark seen on those cows. You ain't told me how many of 'em's yours, if they are, and how they got there."

"Old Brace here told me you said you're afraid to go up in them canyons. Why's that, Sheriff?"

"Ask the pigeon what I said."

Cawley leaned on the bar, turned to Crowell and said, "Tell it like he said it, Brace. This whole place'll be delighted by his words."

Crowell, already caught in the pincers of a maneuvering man, and embarrassment getting its edge in line, said," Sheriff told me up in there ain't no place for us palefaces, 'cause we ain't ones to mess with any of them on our best day. They ain't ever scared of dyin' like we are, us palefaces."

His complexion had gone over to the redness all the way. He swallowed his drink in a hurry, asked for another.

The barkeep, at the other end of the bar, whispered to a couple of old cronies, "Cassidy's the old soldier, you know. Been there and done it all. If I was on a posse, I'd want him leading it. If I was running from it, I'd want him for a saddle pard."

He went up the line and poured a fresh drink for Crowell and whispered over the top of the bottle, "You owe him, son. Be careful where you end up in all of this."

Cassidy put his glass on the bar. "Fill it up, Charlie. I'm going to tell the boys what happened up there in Seven Cave Canyon."

Eyeing both Cawley and Crowell, the sheriff leaned back on the bar and said, "I'm going to tell you a story I ain't told in 30 years or so." He sipped on his drink, nodded at the gathering and the barkeep, and began reciting a long memory.

"I was in C Company of the 5th. Mac Weller was the captain and we trailed some injuns into Seven Cave Canyon. They had rustled some beef from a couple of herds on the way, buffalo gone and the tribes hungry. Along with the cattle they got a bunch of horses, and one hostage, a boy of seven or eight whose father and mother was killed in one of their raids. The Indians went into the canyon and our scouts, two Cherokee from off Oklahoma Territory, stopped right at the edge of the canyon like there was a gate there. No way we could get them to go in there. They said, "The god of Seven Tribes sat just inside with his thunder stick, ready to kill anyone, especially any Indian who didn't come to smoke the peace pipe. Some army scouts were already killed in the canyon, and some men chasing cattle, men from ranches, wagon trains, some freighters who had been robbed in the night and had rushed in there."

"Weller didn't believe any of it. 'All mumbo jumbo,' he said. Some of his troops, been a long time out here in the wars, were skittish, jumping around in the saddle, showing it. Weller got real mad and told me to take a dozen men in there and shake things out for show."

Cassidy took a deep breath, the memories piling up on him. "I swear there was clouds and darkness and god-awful terrible screams coming from all around us like devils were on the loose and looking to cut our legs off or our heads. And the thunder and lightning kept working over us and down between us, cutting us off from each other, and sounding like cannons and bouncing like cats on a hot griddle and three of the men were killed by lightning, burned alive likely. Dead, like shot against a wall by a firing squad.

He paused again, recalled more. "I never heard anything but thunder, screams from a distance, horses sounding like they wanted to high tail it out of there, and the sound of a drum with a cadence so military-like it scared me. And all the time there was this weird sound like cattle on the move, like a stampede was just starting and coming right at us. We dashed to the walls of the canyon for safety. We never saw one cow in there, then or in the morning. The horses were gone. The injuns were gone. Just me in there. Alone. All my men dead … burned alive by lightning, some of them crushed by cattle that wasn't there anymore, and no horses. Them gone too."

Cassidy was into his summary of things, the learning curve bending. "I went in with a dozen men and came out alone. I think they

119

left me alive to carry the message about Seven Cave Canyon, and that's what I'm telling you now."

Silence reined in the saloon until Cawley broke it up. "How can you explain all that stuff, Sheriff? I don't think you can. There's no reasonable way to look at it. No answers."

"There is if you believe in ghosts, spirits, men who can move things like they were never moved. That's the Seven Cave Canyon in there. It's not haunted, if that's what you're thinking ... it's used. It's part of Indian culture. It's their land. It's holy, like I said. I'll bet the cattle Brace saw in there were taken while they were grazing on Indian land. You'd take 'em on your land. Don't tell me you haven't or wouldn't. Then I'd call you a name you won't like. "

Cawley tried to find a way to assert himself. He was grasping at straws. "You don't like me, do you, Sheriff?"

"Cawley," the sheriff said, "there's a whole passel of stuff I don't like about you. Never did. Never will. And you ran the pigeon kid there in to tell me what you wanted me to hear, like an errand boy."

Brace Crowell, embarrassed in front of pals and cronies of long standing, spun about as if he was going to face down the sheriff.

Cassidy, stiffly upright, said, "Cawley, you better wrassle that kid still or he's going dead right in front of you."

He changed his eye target, stared hard at Crowell. "Kid, you can play games with me and lie to me and poke all kinds of fun at me, but don't ever draw down on me or make like you're going to. You're a quick time from dead, kid. I tried to tell you earlier today it was learning time. It looks like maybe you didn't believe me."

Cawley, stepping into the middle of things a little deeper, said, as an aside to the whole saloon, "I've got two men posted out there at the head of the canyon, just to make sure no thieving Indians make some of my cows disappear again. Well, all that says is, I'm settling things my way if the law can't do it. It's all under control now."

It wasn't five minutes later, the saloon occupants trying to settle themselves, enjoy their surroundings, that a rider galloped into town, tied up at the saloon hitch rail, and ran inside, yelling all the way. "Mr. Cawley. Mr. Cawley." He was alarmed, mystified, totally out of breath.

"What the hell is it, Jackson?" Cawley said, still urging Crowell to be calm.

"Nothing's gone in there we could see all day yesterday and last night, 'cause me and Ridley took turns."

"Yeh, so what?" Cawley had his hands on his hips, his eyes reaching around the room for an audience.

"Well, there's a 100 cows in there right now, Mr. Cawley. Yes, sir, 100 at least. I saw 'em. Ridley saw 'em and sent me to tell you. 100 cows." He wiped his brow, tapped his fist on the bar and said to the barkeep, "Give me two jiggers up to the brim." He measured with thumb and forefinger, and tossed two fingers up with the other hand.

Sheriff Tim Cassidy lifted his eyebrows, his eyes staring at Cawley for a response.

There was silence in the saloon. It lasted a long time and ended up carrying the deepest of mysteries that still sit, unanswered, in the Canyon of Seven Caves in Mildred's River Valley.

Now, way off in a dark part of Mildred's River Valley, only an old man, an old Two Kettle Indian, bent and broken in his body, his mind quick as a puma, can offer any solution, but he'll never step forward to talk about Seven Cave Canyon.

ABOUT THE AUTHOR

Tom Sheehan, a 24-time Pushcart Prize nominee, is comfortable writing in several different genres and makes it a point to create each and every day. He's authored the novels *Vigilantes East* and *Death for the Phantom Receiver*. His short story works number *A Collection of Friends*, *From the Quickening*, *Epic Cures, and Brief Cases, Short Spans* in all of which he manages to uncannily include a very special character, his hometown of Saugus, Massachusetts. His eBook releases are *Murder at the Forum* (an NHL novel of Bruins-Canadiens long rivalry), *Death of a Lottery Foe, Death by Punishment*, *An Accountable Death* and *The Westering*, nominated for a National Book Award. Sheehan's poetic ruminations are *Ah, Devon Unbowed*, *The Saugus Book*, *This Rare Earth & Other Flights*, *Reflections from Vinegar Hill* and the eBook *Korean Echoes*, nominated for a Distinguished Military Award. *The Nations* is his first western book.